Eddie Gustafson's
guide to
Christmas
and Other Winter Fun

Eddie Gustafson's

guide to

Christmas

and Other Winter Fun

Dwayne Brenna

COTEAU BOOKS

TWENTY-FIVE YEARS

Edited by Don Kerr.

Cover and interior photos by Brenda Pelkey.
Cover and book design by Duncan Campbell.

Printed and bound in Canada at Transcontinental Printing.

Canadian Cataloguing in Publication Data

Eddie Gustafson's guide to christmas and other winter fun

ISBN 1-55050-171-2

1.Christmas – humor.   2.Norwegian Canadians – Humor.*
I. Title.

PS8553.R3822 E33 2000   C813'.6   C00-920166-1
PR9199.3B6893 E33 2000

1 2 3 4 5 6 7 8 9 10

COTEAU BOOKS
401-2206 Dewdney Ave.
Regina, SK
Canada   S4R 1H3

AVAILABLE IN THE US FROM
General Distribution Services
4500 Witmer Industrial Estates
Niagara Falls, NY, 14305-1386

The publisher gratefully acknowledges the financial assistance of the Saskatchewan Arts Board, the Canada Council for the Arts, the Government of Canada through the Book Publishing Industry Development Program (BPIDP), and the City of Regina Arts Commission, for its publishing program.

Contents

1. Lutefisk and Lefse Sticks

2. Overhand Curling and Other Winter Sports

3. Helga's New Year's Kisses
and Other Wintertime Pleasures

To my Norwegian Grandmother

Velkommen Til Littlestone

Velkommen til Littlestone, pop. 86, as the friendly Viking says on the sign at the Littlestone village limits. Our village is world-famous for lots of things, but if I was pressed to choose one, I'd have to say we're pretty famous for our ground. "Littlestone Loam" is the name the scientists give our soil. It's good for growing wheat, barley, flax, canola, oats, garbanzo beans, pork and beans, and probably even jelly beans. Littlestone Loam gets its fertility from the thousands of metric tonnes of spilled lye it has absorbed during lutefisk soaking season in the last hundred years or so.

We're also famous for the Littlestone and District Henrik Ibsen Drama Festival, which is put on by the pretty widow Freya Sorenson, who lives just a couple of miles south and west of here. (I go out and prune her silver-leaf willows every summer.) The Littlestone and District Henrik Ibsen Drama Festival has attracted reviewers and critics from as far away as Wynyard, Peterson, and Muenster. This year, Freya decided that *Hedda Gabler* would be too dark if Hedda shot herself, so she accidentally missed and the wall was wounded instead.

And we were really famous, until last year, because Elvis appeared on the front of our Credit Union. Not the real Elvis, you understand, just a shadow that was cast upon the stucco of the building when they installed the new street lights on the main drag. Them lights cast a shadow acrost the wall of the building that was the spitting image of Elvis, all dressed up in his figure-skating costume and doing a quadruple sow-cow. Trouble was, Helga Arvinsdatter fell in love with that shadow and accidentally run into the streetlight when she was driving by, and that was the end of Elvis. The King had left the building, as they say.

Now I've decided to put together a little book about Littlestone and the people who live there and how they spend their winters, specially all the fun they have at Christmas (which you can read all about in this book). It ain't exactly a local history, even though everything I say in here is true right down to the last detail. It ain't an article for the Encyclopedia either, cuz I wanted to tell you what the people who live here are really like, not just stuff about the annual rainfall (never enough for the farmers around here) and the major exports (malting barley, garbanzo beans, and recycled tractor batteries). I ain't exactly sure what this book is, but I know what it ain't.

Some of the folks in this book are dear to my heart. There's my faithful dog, Great Western Light, who I had ever since he was a pup and he just keeps showing me new talents every day – like the time he became clairvoyant and got George Swenson and Kristiana Hogdebo hitched. There's my Bestemor (that's Norwegian for "Norwegian grandmother"), who raised me up from an orphan. Bestemor's ninety-two now and still lives out on the farm in a big white house with my Great-aunt Inger. I figure it's the constant games of Norwegian whist that keep them going – or maybe the aquavit they drink while they're playing.

There's the Johannson brothers, Norman and Ingmar and Joe, who is about as different from one another as three brothers can be. Norman, he's my best friend, was ever since we were tykes playing hockey down on the old slough together. Norman farms out there east of town with his good wife Barbo. Norman's slow-talking brother Ingmar is the mayor of Littlestone. Ingmar runs the Hiway Garage out along Number Six. He's got the best collection of rusted-out automobiles you ever seen sitting on his back lot. He could start a museum, no problem. He also likes to invent things. Electrical underwear and pig manure-driven automobiles are two of his best. Norman and Ingmar have a younger brother named Joe, who's always up to some devilment, although he don't say nothing (Joe hasn't said much of anything since that operation he had as a child).

Of course there's also folks who ain't so agreeable, just like any small town, and that would have to include Helga Arvinsdatter. Helga used to go after her husband Arvin something terrible before he went to his Reward, and now she's taken to going after me instead. She lives just down the street from me in a little shingled bungalow, and she's forever trying to get me to do something "fer the good of the community," as she says. It's hard to say no, cuz she's 6'4" and two hundred and sixty pounds of pure meanness, and she wears a man's shoe size thirteen. I suppose she has her good points too – although sometimes you have to look real hard to find them.

But mostly folks is pretty easy to get along with out here.

Wintertime in Littlestone is full of fun so long as you like lutefisk (who don't?) and Ski-Dooing and schmeer in the curling rink. There's also stuff in this book about how we earn our livings and the weather and ice-fishing and Christmas, of course! There ain't too much violence, and the closest we get to sex is when Helga Arvinsdatter tries to plant a kiss full on my lips at the New Year's Dance. So you don't have to be worried about leaving this book around the house in case the children might find it. You can read this book anywheres – in the living room or the kitchen or the summer cookhouse or even the bathroom. (If you read it in the bathroom and don't like it, please wash your hands before sending me a letter of complaint. On second thought, please wash your hands even if you don't send me a letter.)

Wishing You a Happy Winter
  (the best time of year)
    From Me and My Norwegian Grandmother,
      And my friend Norman and his wife Barbo,
      And my Dog Great Western Light,
        Eddie Gustafson
          Box 51
            Littlestone, Sk.

Lutefisk

and

Lefse Sticks

The Rosemalt Lefse Sticks

I SAW NORMAN JOHANNSON AT THE CREDIT Union just before last Christmas. He was coming out of the manager's office, and he looked pretty grim, but he stopped and chatted awhile.

"What's new with you, Eddie?"

I told him that I was driving up to Melfort in three days' time, to try out that new blood pressure machine they have in the Rexall Drugstore there.

"You don't suppose I could catch a ride?" he asked. "I'm lookin' to buy my wife a pair of rosemalt lefse sticks that I seen in the Scandinavian shop."

I drove out to Norman's farm two days later to pick him up. He come out of the garage toting his Eagle Claw rod and Shimano reel. "You plannin' on doin' a little fishing along the way?" I asked him. He tucked the rod in behind the seat of my baby blue pickup, and we took off for Melfort, shooting the breeze and reminiscing about bygone days.

"Remember last Christmas?" I said. "And yer dad, old Johann?"

"Yup. The old feller still believes that lutefisk

is the way to eternal life."

"And also to hardening of the arteries."

Norman stopped smiling then. "There ain't gonna be no lutefisk for Christmas this year, Eddie. Not at our house, anyways."

He didn't have to say no more. I knew that three years in a row of bad harvests must have pretty much ruptured Norman's bank account.

We arrived in Melfort at one in the afternoon. Agreeing to meet me back at the Coach and Three Restaurant at suppertime, Norman got out of the truck. He took his fishing rod with him, and he navigated straight down the sidewalk with a faraway look in his eye, like a farmer opening a new field with a disker.

Turns out there wasn't as big a lineup for the blood pressure machine as I figured there was gonna be. I was all done by 2:30, and I jumped into the baby blue pickup and headed back uptown. When who do I see coming out of a pawnshop with a big smile on his face – but Norman.

I knew then that it was gonna be a merry Christmas after all.

On December twenty-fifth, me and my dog Great Western Light drove out to Norman's farm and so we had the opportunity to observe true love in action and also to see what Norman and his wife Barbo had bought for one another. First they gave me a present, which was a nice box of peppermint patties – my favourite! Then I gave them a present, which was a bag of Oh Henry bars – said it was from me and the dog.

Then Barbo opened her gift. Her nimble fingers tore into the long package until the lefse sticks were in plain view. She let out a squeal of delight and then a whimper. "Oh, Norman, these are beautiful. But I sold the lefse griddle to buy your present."

She handed a nicely wrapped package to Norman and he opened it. He looked at the Mepps spinners thoughtfully for a long time. "Let's just set these presents aside for awhile."

"What's the matter, Norman?"

"Truth is, I pawned the fishing rod to buy your lefse sticks."

Now, I don't know about you but, as for me and my dog, we tend to agree with what O. Henry said, when he wasn't busy making chocolate bars: of all the wise people in the world, people like Norman and Barbo are the wisest.

Martin Luther
Was a Norwegian

US NORSKIES DECORATE OUR CHRISTMAS trees in a very particular manner, and I'm here to tell you just exactly how we do it.

First off, we go out in the Barrier River Valley or somewheres and chop down the perfect tree. It can be a pine or a blue spruce or a white spruce – it doesn't matter – the important thing is that you use an axe and not a Swede saw. Norwegians and Swedes have never gotten along all that well, and rumour has it that Swedes invented those awkward saws so that unsuspecting Norwegians would cut themselves.

It's important to strap the Christmas tree to the roof of the baby blue pickup and to drive home at speeds in excess of seventy miles per hour. This blows the lint and birds' nests out of the branches – and also any loose pine needles. If your tree arrives home without any needles at all, completely and shamelessly nude, it either wasn't meant to be a Christmas tree in the first place or else it's a crafty little poplar that's been masquerading as an evergreen.

Once the tree is at home, most regular people mount it in a Christmas tree holder filled with sugary water. Not Norskies, though. We stand our trees up in a vat of melted butter, which percolates through the branches and gives the needles a silky shine. You got to be careful not to spill any melted butter on the tree, though, because hungry Norwegians will eat anything – Christmas trees and fenceposts included – if it's soaked in melted butter long enough.

Which is also why you never pour melted butter over the popcorn that you make to string around the tree.

There is a long list of decorations that us Norwegians must have on our trees. The most important item on the list is the string of miniature Norwegian flags, all bright red and blue, which colourfully festoons the Christmas tree in every self-respecting Norwegian's house. That's in case you drink so much aquavit on Christmas Eve that you accidentally forget where you come from.

There's also the ornamental cross-country skier telemarking down the slopes of some Norwegian mountain or other. Skiing is the second most popular sport of Norwegians, next to overhand curling, and so it is only right that a skier should hang from the tree.

In the course of the Christmas season, photographs of long-lost relatives back in Norway arrive in the homes of most Norwegian Canadians. We frame them in cardboard and hang them from the Christmas tree. Oh, you've all seen them – photos of unsmiling elderly relatives with shaggy moustaches and bushy eyebrows – and that's just the women. My dog Great Western Light took such a torrid dislike to one of them photographs one time that he refused to pee on the Christmas tree till after New Year's Day, when all the decorations had been taken off.

The ornamental church that plays "Silent Night" is also a fixture on many Norwegian Christmas trees. The composer of "Silent Night," Martin Luther, was a famous Norwegian – yes, he was! – he loved to walk in the snow and he couldn't sing worth a darn – which is one reason why he didn't record his own songs. It's no big deal, though, because Norwegians prefer to hear Olaf Sven sing their Christmas carols for them.

A long-nosed troll stands underneath the Norwegian Christmas tree. Most Norwegians will tell you that the troll is a popular figure in our mythology and that trolls have ruined many a Christmas by kidnapping the children of merrymakers. But that's not why the troll is part of the Christmas decorations every year. No, the real reason is that many Norwegians are terrible short of storage space because they use their garages to soak their lutefisk in, and so they must keep their lawn ornaments under the tree until summer comes back.

Potatoes and Christmas
Lights Don't Mix

"**H**AND ME UP THAT THERE STRING OF Christmas lights," I said to my friend Ingmar Johannson. "But be careful." Fussiness about not breaking things ain't one of Ingmar's personality traits; he busted three of the bulbs just getting that string of lights out of the cardboard box – and they were the good kind that twinkles through the Christmas frost like stars in the winter sky.

Ingmar shot me a look whilst he was breaking them bulbs. "You should do this in November," he said. He took his mitts off and blew on his fingers.

"Why? So's I can keep up with the Arvins-datters? I ain't one of those that believes in celebrating Christmas before Halloween's over."

"And you should use a good stepladder."

"This ladder is solid as the day I built it. Why, I tightened up the braces on her just last summer before I –" Out of a surly sense of Christmas hum-buggery, the stepladder commenced collapsing just then, landing me on my keester in the rock garden by my driveway.

"See," Ingmar drawled in a smirky way.

"Enough to give a gopher the heartburn," I said. "If you ain't interested in helping me put these Christmas lights up on my house, why'nt you just go home?"

"Jah, but who will drive you to the hospital after?"

I made a few minor repairs to the ladder and got it set back up, then I commenced stringing them lights all along the eavestroughs. "Okey-dokey now," I told Ingmar, "if yer not too busy doin' yer impression of a ice sculpture, maybe you can take that extension cord and plug it into the outlet on the side of the garage."

It only took Ingmar about fifteen minutes to find the outlet, and then those lights commenced twinkling like the eyes of Skadi's father – all except for them three bulbs that Ingmar had busted. I tried to twist one of the broken lights out of its socket, first with my mitts on, then with my mitts off, and then with a pair of pliers. "She's in there good and tight," I complained to Ingmar. "But I got a trick that'll get a discombobulated Christmas light out of a socket every time, slicker than a garter snake through a Massey Harris combine on garbanzo bean setting."

We went into the house, and I got a netted gem potato out of the fridge. "See this," I said to Ingmar, once we were back outside, "you just grind the potato into the broken bulb like this, and then you give her a twist. I learned this by watching that home improvement show on TV."

That's when I learned two other things. First, that you should always unplug your Christmas lights before you try your amazing potato trick that you saw on TV. Second, that potatoes conduct electricity pretty good, probably because of all the moisture they got in them. Ingmar, he was so startled, he just stood there like a decoy in duck-hunting season. I probably would have been on that ladder getting myself electrinated till the cows came home if the ladder hadn't fallen apart again from all the shaking and if I hadn't fallen offa it.

But every cloud has a silver lining at Christmastime. And with all the blood vessels that burst in my head from the electric shock, I was so red in the face for the next couple of weeks that I made a real convincing Santa Claus at the Littlestone Lutheran Church Christmas party. And by New Year's, I was able to walk again without the use of a cane.

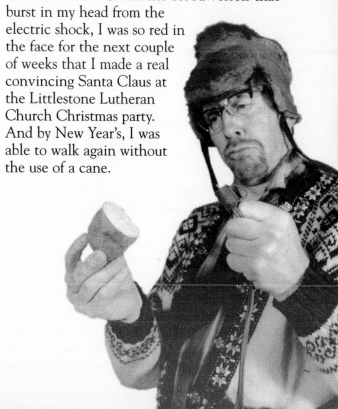

Delivering
Washing Machines

NORMAN JOHANNSON AND ME HAVE BEEN suffering from the cabin fever ever since the local pool hall closed down. So we decided to take a job at the Co-op store during the Christmas season, delivering groceries and hardware in the Co-op half-ton.

It's a good job. You get to deliver presents and Christmas goodies, and everybody's happy to see you. If you have time to stop for a minute, they invite you in for coffee or tea or something stronger. And the money's going to come in handy – seventy-five bucks a day – even though Norman's doing better this year than last (he had a whole field of barley go malting, so he was able to buy back his fishing rod and his lefse griddle from the pawnshop).

There's a few things you've gotta look out for, though, when you're Co-op Store delivery men. One is the Liehn boys, who skip out of high school so they can lay in wait for the delivery truck. They know the heater in that old Chev is broken and won't turn off, so we have to keep the windows partly open. And they hide in back alleys and behind buildings so they can jump out at the right moment and pelt us with snowballs. I took a snowball in the side of the head one afternoon. My eardrum's still thawing out.

The other thing you have to look out for is old Mrs. Nordstrum's dog Minchie. Now, you may know that I love dogs when they're big and intelligent like my own Great Western Light. But Mrs. Nordstrum's dog is a bulldog with a pushed-in face and a cranky look in its eye, kinda like Mrs. Nordstrum herself. But that's another story.

Anyway, Norman and me were in the store one fine day just before Christmas, sampling the cashews, when the call come out for us to deliver a new Kenmore washing machine to Mrs. Nordstrum's place, up there on Boundary Avenue. Mrs. Nordstrum's daughter Nora, who lives in Saskatoon with her husband now, had phoned up and paid for it with her credit card and asked for it to be delivered as a Christmas present. So Norman and me loaded it up in the truck and off we went, keeping an eye out along the way for the Liehn kids.

But there were no snowballs that day, so I mighta known something worse was just over the horizon. We pulled up in front of Mrs. Nordstrum's house and started unloading the washer.

Those Kenmores can be pretty heavy. But Norman and me got it outta the box of the truck and we were making our way through foot-deep snow to Mrs. Nordstrum's front door. She doesn't have a sidewalk, Mrs. Nordstrum, only a foot-path, so you can't fault her for not shovelling it.

Then the front door flies open and the old

lady is out there on the step, asking us what we think we're doin' and telling us that she didn't order no washing machine. And her dog Minchie is letting off his high-pitched yelp and nipping at Norman's heel. Norman is straining under the weight of that Kenmore (he just had a hernia operation last year), but he takes the time to hiss at the dog, "Get away ya mutt! Go on with ya!" But the dog won't leave him alone.

I'm standing half-in and half-out of the house, trying to explain how this machine is a gift from Nora, when I look over at Norman. He has that look of despair he sometimes gets when his brother Joe accidentally burns down one of his granaries. And he's gawking down at his pant leg. That darn dog has drawn up beside him and is urinating all over Norman's new coveralls. Norman can't hardly move, but he's dancing a little of the old St. Vitus, and all he can say is "Keesh-ta!" as that little varmint goes about his business. I truly wished Great Western Light was there to chase the mangy critter away.

Being as it was Christmastime, of course, peace and harmony prevailed. The old lady was so tickled to be getting a new washing machine – free – that she invited us both in for gammelost and some of her tapioca beer. She forced Norman to take his coveralls off and she washed them up in her new machine. The first load, she said, was in Norman's honour. After a few glasses of that tapioca beer, Norman and me developed a new appreciation for old Mrs. Nordstrum and we wished her the best of the season. The coveralls had dried by that time, so Norman put them on and we headed out the door. But I noticed that Norman couldn't resist accidentally kicking Minchie off the step when we went outside.

I guess you can't pee on a man's pant leg and pretend you're friends with him afterwards.

Co-op Store Santa

I SUPPOSE THERE'S SOME GOOD IN EVERY KID, if you look hard enough, although a Co-op store Santa Claus sometimes has to look real hard.

When the manager of the Co-op, Henry Skogsrud, asked me to masquerade as good ole Saint Nick this Christmas season (since there wasn't as much delivery work as he thought there was going to be), I thought it sounded a little too much like hard labour. When he informed me that he was paying ten dollars an hour to the first fella who would wear the grey beard and the red toque, I got over my antipathy for the job and agreed to participate wholeheartedly.

Everything was just fine and dandy after that – I spent entire days teasing little children and telling them what they might and might not get for Christmas. Until it was the twenty-first of December and Mrs. Shelley Holmerud brought her six-year-old son Haakon into town to sit on my knee. "The boy needs a father figure in his life," she whispered to me. "Ever since Eric" – that's her husband – "ever since Eric went to the oilpatch this fall, young Haakon has been starved for male attention."

It's a sad, sad story, and one which has been told often enough in these parts, of the young farmer who is forced to leave the farm and the family every autumn and to go westward in search of employment so that he might subsidize his meagre farm income. Shelley's eyes commenced turning red. "Eric just called again last night. Said he wouldn't likely be home on Christmas Day neither, because they're offerin' time-and-a-half if you roughneck on the holidays. It's too good to pass up, is what he said."

"Come sit on old Santa's knee!" I exclaimed, pointing directly at young Haakon. "Yer not ascared of good ole Kris Kringle, are you?"

"I ain't ascared," the boy said. "I just don't like you much, that's all."

"Well, now, how is Santa s'posed to know what to get you fer Christmas, if you won't sit on his knee?"

"I'll tell you from here, that's good enough."

I could see that the dear child was starved for male attention all right, especially the kind of attention that results in a warm backside.

"Yer not the real Santa Claus, anyway," the boy said. "I know you. Yer that old guy with the funny hat that plays schmeer in the rink all the time."

"No, as a matter of fact, that's my long-lost Norwegian cousin." I gave the kid a steely look. "So whattaya want fer Christmas?"

"As if you could get it for me."

"I might."

"Have you got a cigarette? You could give me

that for Christmas, and maybe I'd be happy."

A cigarette! A six-year-old boy smoking cigarettes! This child was an atheist and a non-believer in Santa Claus and a smoker of cigarettes to boot! I had half a mind to let him have a taste of my chewing tobacco, just to teach him a lesson, but then I noticed the front door of the store swing open. And there stood big Eric Holmerud, his hair sticking up and his face all ruddy.

The boy turned and saw his father. All the rudeness left his face that minute, and he was a six-year-old boy again – not some dwarf teenager who didn't believe in Santa Claus. "Dad!" young Haakon shouted, and he went veering across the wet tile floor towards his father. Big Eric scooped the boy up in one arm and hugged his wife with the other.

"I thought you weren't able to come home for Christmas," said young Shelley.

"To heck with overtime wages," Eric replied. "A man's gotta see his family once in awhile."

After some hugging and some kissing, they all came back to where I was sitting. "Is the boy gonna get what he wants for Christmas, this year, Santa?" Eric asked me. "Or has he been good enough?"

"Oh, they're all good deep down to the undermost places of their hearts," I told him. "And I think young Haakon'll get just what he wants fer Christmas."

Norwegian Whist

ALWAYS ON THE EVENING OF DECEMBER twenty-third, there's a traditional game of Norwegian whist that pits me and my card partner Norman against Bestemor and Great-aunt Inger. Moneywise, the stakes ain't high – we play for a penny a trick and a nickel per game. But there's a lot of pride that's won and lost in those card games. At the end of the evening, my Great-aunt Inger always offers me a cashew or a licorice allsort and says, "Thanks for the card game...loser!" Then my Bestemor and my great-aunt clap their hands together in a high five. Sometimes, they do a little victory dance that they learned from watching CFL football on television.

This year, I suggested to Norman that the only way we could win was to cheat.

"Cheat!" he sputtered. "Against two old ladies. We don't even cheat against the boys playin' schmeer down at the rink."

"Do you wanna make some money before Christmas or don't you?"

"Well, yeah."

"Then here's what you do. If you've got a mitt-ful of clubs, you tell a joke and then surreptitiously knock on the table in the manner of hitting something with a club. If you've got diamonds, scratch your ring finger – like this. If it's hearts you want me to lead in, cough and pound on your chest like you're havin' a heart attack. If it's spades, you hum that song from Snow White and the Seven Dwarfs: 'Hi ho, hi ho, hi ho, it's off to work we go....' But you gotta be discreet, because my old Bestemor's pretty observant behind those bifocals of hers."

After supper, on the evening of the twenty-third, we cleared the dishes off the old oak table, got out Bestemor's deck of cards for the short-sighted, and started playing. Norman and me were coughing, scratching, knocking, and singing like variety entertainers on the *Ed Sullivan Show,* and in that fashion we managed to win the first hand.

"Let's up the ante, Auntie. How about we play for ten cents a trick and a dollar a hand?"

"Oh, I don't know. Isn't that too much like gambling?"

"Are you chicken?"

"Only God-fearing."

My great-auntie's religious, but I also know that she doesn't like to back down when it comes to a card game challenge. "Are you scared we're gonna whup ya?"

"All right, smartie pants. Ten cents a trick and a dollar a hand it is."

In the middle of the second hand, Bestemor commenced screwing up her face like she was thinking real hard. Then she threw her cards down on the table and she said, "Eddie, I see what you're doing. Scratching on the ring finger for diamonds, knocking on the table for clubs – that kind of cheating is for sloskins and it won't be tolerated here."

"What? Norman and me weren't cheating."

"Yes, we were. And it was all Eddie's idea."

"My idea!"

"Yup. But why don't we go back and replay the first hand, just in the name of fairness."

After that, Norman and me lost at seven successive hands of whist. My dog Western Light was so tired and bored of watching us being soundly trounced that he crawled under the table and went to sleep. But he wasn't having a sound dognap. Every now and then, I'd hear him muttering and whimpering as though he was dreaming of having porcupine quills pulled out of his muzzle.

In the middle of the next hand of cards, I quietly leaned back in my chair to get a better look at what was going on under the table. There was Western Light sawing logs, and there was my great-aunt Inger kicking him in the ribs. The dog would whimper every time she dug her slippered toe into him. Sometimes he'd let out one long whimper, sometimes two or three short ones.

Who would have expected two Norwegian octogenarians to be cheating at cards? I was so dumbfounded that I didn't say anything – not until we were nearly finished the game. Then I turned to my great-aunt. "The way I see it, you've either developed a nervous tic during the course of this card game or else you've got some animosity towards canines. Maybe you could tell me which it is."

"What are you talking about, Eddie?"

"All those kicks under the table, all those foot signals you're tryin' to make. Cheating is the worst form of dishonesty as far as I'm concerned."

"Now don't say anything you'll regret later," my Norwegian grandmother cut in.

"What about all the money we been losing to ya?" There was at least twenty dollars on the table in front of her.

"We'll play one more hand. Double or nothing. Or maybe you're just plain chicken?"

"Okay, but first we put a leaf in the table so you two can't play footsie!"

"Så, gå og legg deg ňo, så ot lusa kan få mat," said Great-aunt Inger (that's Norwegian for something I can't repeat here).

After I'd put a leaf in the table, we played the final hand. A quiet descended when the cards were dealt. With each successive trick, the tension grew more and more unbearable. When the game ended, my great-auntie offered me a cashew. "Thanks for the card game...loser!" And she leaped out of her chair, grabbed my grandma by the hand, and they danced the combined victory dance of Donald Narcisse and Daniel Farthing.

Norwegians Is the
World's Worst Singers

I DON'T KNOW WHAT GETS INTO NORWE-
GIANS when they go to church on Sunday
mornings, but they either become the
world's loudest snorers or the world's worst
singers. And I'm convinced that the Littlestone
Lutheran Church has the finest collection of
both.

Last Sunday, I had the misfortune of sitting
behind Semi Knudsen and his wife Hanna, there
at the back of the church.

Preacher Nelson hadn't even got past the
Epistle lesson and into the sermon before those
two started nodding off. First Semi's bald head
began to droop, and then Hanna followed suit.
And then they started to breathe kinda hoarse.
Pretty soon, they both just threw their heads
back and caution to the winds, mouths wide
open, and started snoring fit to wake the devil.

Lucky the devil wasn't on the premises that
day.

And if Semi and Hanna's snoring isn't
enough, we've got the choir to sing for us.

Now I read somewhere that the Japanese
have a different tonal scale than our own. Their

notes don't have any resemblance to what we think of as the normal "do-re-mi-fa-so-la-ti-do." Well, I've got a theory. And my theory is that the Church Choir in Littlestone is the only choir in the Western world that had enough gumption to learn that Japanese scale off by heart and to adapt all our hymns to it.

Awful! Let me tell you. You'd think that outta twenty-two people, somebody'd be able to sing in the right key!

But the worst moment in the history of the Littlestone Church – or in the history of music for that matter – was when Helga Arvinsdatter stepped out of the choir to perform a solo. It was last Christmas, and she decided to bless us with her rendition of "Silent Night." She tore into that song, screechin' away at the top of her lungs. And I coulda sworn I heard some distant voice trying to harmonize with her. So I listened carefully and, sure enough, it was my dog Great Western Light. He was three blocks away at the time – in my backyard – but he still heard Helga's high-pitched squeal as clear as a dog whistle. And he was protesting with his own plaintive howl the massive assault she was making on his ears.

There was Helga singin' "Si-i-lent Ni-i-ght! Ho-o-ly Ni-i-ight!" And there was Great Western Light, five or six hundred yards away, howling, "Aaaaaaaah aaaaah!"

At Eastertime, Preacher Nelson announced that he had a special treat for us – a chamber choir come all the way from Missouri.

Now I figure these people knew what they

they were doing. They had a conductor. And a soprano section. And an alto section. And a bass section. And they sang tunes that weren't even in our hymn book.

I thoroughly enjoyed it.

As I was leaving church that day, Helga Arvinsdatter caught me by the arm. And she whispered, "Eddie, tell me if I'm wrong, but wasn't that chamber choir a little bit off key?"

I suppose a better man might have spoke the truth and shamed the devil. Specially since we were in church. All I could muster was: "Yes, Helga, I don't think they've mastered the intricacies of the Japanese tonal scale yet."

And then I bade her good day.

Lutefisk Is an Aphrodisiac

IT'S WELL KNOWN THAT LUTEFISK IS GOOD for many things, including constipation, black fly repellent, and smearing on the underbellies of airplanes when they have to make a landing without landing gear. But a little-known fact about lutefisk is that it's a powerful aphrodisiac.

Of course, us Norskies have known about the amorous properties of lutefisk all along. In our popular folktales, there's a mysterious figure by the name of Orvis who had an unfortunate encounter with a gaggle of Hollingdal women on their way back from a Christmas feed of lutefisk. It seems these women were so het up that they caught young Orvis by the collar and tried to hug and kiss him. But they were unseasonably greedy between themselves, and they ended up ripping young Orvis apart, limb by limb. Then they threw his head over a big waterfall called the Hollingvossen. But Orvis was heard to sing, in a most melodious voice, as his noggin went over the falls. And the song he sung went like this:

> *"Lefse, gammelost, hva skal du ha?*
> *Lutefisk! Lutefisk! ja! ja! ja!"*

It was a touching little ditty. And I discovered its true meaning two Christmases ago, at the Littlestone and District Chamber of Commerce Annual Lutefisk Supper, which was held in the Town Hall. Oh, we all chowed down real good, never thinking that our gluttony was gonna lead to a worse sin by the end of the evening!

The Ladies Aid was in the kitchen, washing off the stovetops with bleach – which is just about the onliest way to get rid of the pungent aroma of freshly boiled lutefisk other than to repaint your interior walls. The lutefisk had been eaten, and the Johnsons and the Olsens and the Hagebloms were all wiping the melted butter off their faces and teetering towards the door. I felt that it would be a fitting gesture on my part to go into the kitchen and express my appreciation to the ladies for yet another successful lutefisk dinner. It never occurred to me that those ladies had been breathing lutefisk fumes since mid-afternoon and that they had been sampling the lutefisk all evening to make sure that it was cooked just right.

Well, sir, by the time I walked into that kitchen, you could hear the female pheromones bouncing off the cupboards. They had the cassette tape player going in there, and it was playing an Olaf Sven recording of Styrrmansvalsen. And I could tell those ladies were all fantasizing about the Styrrman.

"Thanks, ladies," I said, looking at no one in particular. "That was a darn good meal."

"You are a sweet, sweet man," said Freya

Sorenson, with a dreamy look in her eye. "How would you like a second helping?"

"Go ahead, Eddie," Helga Arvinsdatter added. "It'll put lead in yer pencil." The other ladies let out a giggle.

"Well, I gotta go."

Helga caught me firmly by the arm. "Not so fast, Eddie, we're not done with you yet. Just you sit down on this here chair. We're gonna give you a special treat. But first you gotta give us each a New Year's kiss."

"It ain't New Year's yet!" I protested.

But it was too late.

When I come outta that kitchen an hour or so later, my Hollingdal cardigan was tore nearly to shreds and I had lipstick imprints on ninety-five percent of my body.

Never Look Your Norwegian Grandmother in the Mouth

WHEN I WAS A YOUNG SPROUT GROWING up, I received a pair of handknit woolen mittens every year at Christmas. On the day the presents first were set under the tree, there would always be a soft parcel from Bestemor. If you felt the package long enough, you could generally locate the thumb of the mitten. My heart usually fell at that moment. Why, oh why, couldn't Bestemor get me something that rattled around tinnily inside a box – like, maybe, a toy logging truck with little logs that you could load and unload.

Come Christmas Eve, I would open my gift of mittens with a look of feigned surprise. I would thank my grandmother, and then I would go have endless fun playing with my new present. Sometimes, I would use the mittens as hand puppets and improvise stories about little boys who got just what they wanted for Christmas. Sometimes, I would go and play outside, and then I'd fill my new mittens with snow and hurl them like grenades at the barn door. That was no end of excitement! One Christmas, I even found a way to put the mittens on my ears, and I went braying around Bestemor's farmyard like a forlorn donkey chasing a carrot that was always a foot out of reach.

In my fifteenth year, the joy of receiving my annual pair of mittens was finally too much for me. As I began to open my present, I mumbled something about hoping it wasn't mittens again this year.

"What? What did you say?"

"I said, 'I hope it isn't mittens again.'"

"Oh? And what would you like instead?"

"I dunno. Something hard, that rattles around inside a factory-made box."

"Fine. Perhaps next year, that is just what you'll get."

The next year, just before Christmas, Bestemor slipped a square box, nicely wrapped in tissue paper, under the tree. I spent a week massaging it and shaking it, smelling it and listening to it. Something was rattling around in there, sure enough, and I had many happy hours imagining a harmonica or a pair of binoculars or a moose call. On Christmas Day, I tore into the wrapping paper with teenage fervour, and inside the box I found – a piece of coal, a lonesome piece of coal. "And that," said Bestemor, "is what happens when boys complain about their Christmas presents."

For the next forty years, Bestemor included a lump of coal with every Christmas gift she gave me. Oh, she'd always supply a real present to go along with the coal – usually some store-bought trinket like cufflinks or a cowboy bow tie, but never mittens. I wasn't unhappy, even though I knew those cufflinks and bow ties were picked off the rack in the local Macleod's store. I figured I already had a lifetime supply of homemade mittens anyways.

So this Christmas, me and Western Light were on our way out to Bestemor's farm. She lives twelve miles from town, and sure enough, out in the middle of nowheres, my baby blue pickup truck got a flat tire. I reached behind the seat for the last pair of woolen mittens my grandmother had knitted for me. They were a little too small, and the palms of those mittens were worn almost clean through. I nearly froze my hands trying to get the lug nuts off the rim. It took me an hour and a half to finish changing the tire, what with the freezing temperatures. I arrived at Bestemor's house, blowing on my fingertips and complaining.

"Well, this year's present should come in handy then." She pressed a large box into my cramped blue hands. With numb fingers, I opened it. Inside there was a lump of coal – and forty pairs of mittens handknit by my Norwegian grandmother.

"Well, thank you, Bestemor! This is the best present ever."

"I figure you've learned your lesson by now. No more complaining about your Christmas presents, eh?"

"No more complaining," I said, as I lifted my mittened hands in the air. I had learned my lesson: you should never look a gift from your grandmother in the mouth. You should never look your grandmother in the mouth either, for that matter – especially if she hasn't got her teeth in.

Archie McPherson's
Lutefisk Dinner

NOWADAYS WE ALWAYS EAT PREPARED lutefisk that's been processed and freeze-dried and packaged in boxes. But I prefer lutefisk the way they made it in the old days. That was lutefisk with a real tang to it. My Norwegian grandmother and my great-aunt Inger are just about the onliest people I know who still lute their own fisk.

The making of old-time lutefisk is a delicate matter. It all begins at some fisherman's shack on the western coast of Norway, where the fish has been snatched from the sea and where it's pickled in lye for six-and-one-half years. Old-fashioned lutefisk comes in small wooden barrels, shipped across the Atlantic and then transported overland by the CNR. When it arrives in Saskatchewan, I always get a call from my Bestemor and from my great-aunt Inger. "We're going to wash the lye out of the fish today. Won't you come and help? Or are you still mad at us for beating you at cards?"

I show up at Bestemor's farm with a two-gallon milk pail. I fill the pail with tap water and dump in the dried cod. The water bubbles and gurgles for the next seven weeks – Bestemor tells me that the lye is coming out of the fish and causing a reaction something like the Chernobyl meltdown. A few days before Christmas, Bestemor deposits the fish into an old hairnet or a woolen sock and boils it to within an inch of its life.

For a Norwegian, lutefisk is as much a part of Christmas as presents, Jule Niesse, and Sunday School skits about Martin Luther. But for non-Norwegians, the consumption of lutefisk is a different matter. Last Christmas, Bestemor had invited Archie McPherson, the local Credit Union manager, out to the farm for dinner. I could tell he didn't know what to make of the lutefisk. "Och, looks like tripe."

"It's just fish," I told him. "Dig in."

Bestemor has boasted more than once that if a man has courage enough to swallow the first bite of her lutefisk, he'll be hooked for life after that. She claims that she shamelessly lured my grandfather into marriage with just such a Christmas treat. Archie managed to gulp down the first mouthful, and then he couldn't help himself. He didn't even notice (as some do) that the silverware was turning black after the first helping – a discoloration caused by the small amounts of lye that couldn't be washed out of the codfish. After the second helping, however, the silverware was as smoky as burned stubble.

"Shame on you, Archie," I teased him. "You've gnawed the silver coating right offa my grandma's cutlery."

Archie's voice had dropped two octaves by the time he was halfway through his fourth helping. My great-aunt asked him how he got started in the banking business.

"I was havin' brekkie wi' me father, one bra mornin', and he said, 'Archie, money maks the world go 'round.'"

At the end of the meal, Archie got up to recite "Auld Lang Syne" or something. He opened his mouth, but no words came out. The rest of us tried to speak. No one could make a sound. Even my dog, who'd eaten a helping of the Christmas fish, was trying to bark, but he couldn't. We hadn't soaked the lutefisk long enough to wash the lye out of it!

I herded everyone into the baby blue pickup and we headed for the hospital in Watson. Inside the truck cab, we were all pretty wide-eyed. We were wondering if we'd ever speak again, and Bestemor was feeling badly for poisoning us on a religious holiday. I don't know if you've ever swallowed lye before, but it begins to feel like you've performed a tonsillectomy on yourself with a butane lighter. You don't know whether to call the doctor or the fire department.

When we arrived at the hospital, crusty old Doctor Gudbrudson chuckled and said, "Eddie, I never thought I'd witness an occasion on which you'd be speechless." He laughed, but I didn't. Then he produced five stomach pumps and proceeded to shove plastic hoses down our throats.

It was truly a Christmas to remember.

Last week, I happened to be in the Credit Union on business, and I said to Archie, "By the way, are you planning to come out to my grandma's this year and help us celebrate Christmas?"

"Not on your life!" he said. "This year, I'm stayin' home wi' ma haggis."

Johann Johannson's Christmas

CHRISTMAS IS A TIME OF PEACE AND fellowship and religiosity, of getting together with friends for hayrides and bonfires, of ice fishing, kissing under the mistletoe, and various other indoor activities. But I can't help worrying about old men who eat lutefisk despite all of that.

Every Christmas, my friend Norman Johannson invites me and my dog Great Western Light for a swell family dinner at his house. Norman's good wife Barbo always cooks up something a little special for Western Light – maybe a pork chop or a drumstick or some such. And for the rest of us, she makes a traditional Norwegian Christmas dinner.

She usually starts getting ready for this meal in mid-October, when she dusts off the griddle, mashes some potatoes, mixes in the flour, rolls out the whole concoction, and cooks it up into what we call lefse. When you apply a liberal amount of butter and sugar or Roger's Golden Syrup, Barbo's super-soft lefse tastes about as good as a thing can taste. And three days before Christmas, Barbo goes into town and buys two boxes of lutefisk at the local Co-op. She thaws it, spends most of a day cooking it, then she drowns those tender white flakes of cod in melted butter and serves it up.

I've seen people change their nationalities and declare themselves Norwegian after one taste of Barbo's lutefisk. And she also makes a jellied salad of some sort, topped with whipped cream. And a buttery Christmas cake with icing three inches thick. There's nuts and Christmas candy on the coffee table and eggnog to drink.

So how could I be anxious on an occasion like this? Well, the problem is Norman's dad Old Johann Johannson, who's about ninety and still farms out in the back country there, west of Archerwill. On the morning of the twenty-fourth, Norman and his brothers Ingmar and Joe take the half-ton out to Johann's homestead and pick the old fella up, and haul him back to Norman's for the Christmas dinner.

Old Johann has a bad case of hardening of the arteries, but that doesn't stop him. He gorges down the Christmas meal, eating extra helpings of lutefisk soaked in butter, and speaking half in Norwegian, half in English until you can't understand a word he's saying. Then he'll stop yammering just as he's lifting another forkful to his mouth, and he'll sit there all quiet for a good two minutes. And then a bead of sweat'll trickle down his forehead and run down to the tip of his nose. And his eyes'll glaze over and his breathing will get kind of heavy. That's when the rest of us usually notice. So Norman, Ingmar, Joe, and I get up and lift the old man out of his chair, very carefully, and lay him down again on the sofa in Norman's living room. We put a pillow under his head and get on the blower to the doctor in Watson.

It normally takes Doc Gudbrudson exactly forty-five minutes to drive from his home to Norman's. And before he gets there, old Johann comes to again with all his grandchildren making a fuss over him. Pretty soon, the old man gets up and demands that we play his favourite Olaf Sven recording of "Life in the Finland Woods" on the phonograph. Barbo has to dance with him. And by the time the doctor gets there, old Johann is standing in the doorway with a bottle in one hand and a cup in the other. When the doctor asks to examine him, Johann says, "Du må ta et glass aquavit først." So the doctor takes a drink and pretty soon we're all up dancing and old Johann's checkup's gonna have to wait another year.

Cousin Elmer's Christmas Card

IT'S COMMON KNOWLEDGE, I GUESS, THAT US Norskies is an unhappy bunch. Might have something to do with living for too many years in a cold and unforgiving landscape. I don't know why, but if you put a bunch of Norwegians together at Christmastime they're just as apt to end up crying as laughing.

And the Christmas cards that Norwegians send to each other ain't exactly filled with joy and good humour. Other folks is writing their relatives bragging about their kids or their new car. But Norwegians put in their cards how their arthritis is acting up or how the housecat froze to the front step.

I got a late Christmas card and letter from my cousin Elmer Hogdebo just the other day. (He'd forgotten to put a stamp on it.) This is what it said:

Dear Eddie,

I hope you are doing fine.

It has been a good year for me.

In February, I learned that I have a daughter I never knew I had. She wrote me a letter from the Correctional Facility in Prince Albert. 'You don't know me,' she said, 'my name is Susie Hogdebo and you are my father. I am twenty-eight years old. My mother was Sharon Torgenson of Archerwill.'

It was so pleasing to learn that I am the father of a bouncing baby girl, especially as my union with wife Agnes has been childless these last forty years.

Agnes was not as pleased as I was to hear from the girl. 'If the young lady is now twenty-eight,' she said, 'that means she was born in 1971.'

'Yes, and all this time I thought I was without offspring.'

'You been married to me,' she said, 'since 1960.'

'Oh.'

'So what were you up to in 1971 that you got a daughter?'

You know, Eddie, the hardest thing to explain to your wife is that you have been secretly donating samples to the sperm bank for many years. 'They must have used one of them samples,' I told her.

'I don't believe you,' she said. And just to make her point, she went into the bedroom and packed her suitcases.

'Where are you going?' I asked.

'To Sintaluta,' she said. 'Home to Mother.'

Since Agnes left me, I have had plenty of

time to write letters to my new daughter. I have also rekindled a lifelong interest in whittling!

Farming is going well. The Credit Union now owns all of my land, but they are quite happy to rent it back to me. My combine gave up the ghost last fall, after thirty-five years of good service. So I only have to come up with a hundred thousand dollars between now and next autumn. Maybe I can sell my whittling, once I get real good at it.

So you see, life has been good to me this year. I hope it has been good to you also.

With a firm handshake,

Cousin Elmer

I didn't know what to write Elmer in return, but I sent him a brand new whittling knife and wished him a Happy New Year.

A Littlestone Nativity

I HAD A STRANGE DREAM ON CHRISTMAS EVE. Maybe I shouldn't have accepted that last glass of aquavit which Norman offered me. Ingmar gets the stuff direct from Oslo, and there's no telling what they put into it there. But every Norwegian knows that aquavit gives you bad gas and fanciful dreams.

I don't remember who drove me home or who tucked me into bed. But round about three in the morning, I awoke and found myself in Norman's cow pasture with my faithful Western Light and Norman's brothers Ingmar and Joe. We seemed to be searching through a forest of poplar for Norman's lost cattle. "C'boss! C'boss!" But no cattle mooed in reply.

Then we walked into a clearing and there, lit by a thousand moonbeams in the falling snow, was an angel. She must have been an angel. She was wearing a brushed velvet Hardanger dress. Her hair was golden. She was singing the Norwegian national anthem:

> *"Ja vi elsker dette landet*
> *Som det stiger frem…."*

Her song ended. "This night," she said, "the boy child Jesu is born in Bethlehem. Go seek him there." She glided backwards into the poplar glade and disappeared.

"Who's this Jesu?"

"Beats me. Couldn't have been born in these parts or he'd have a name like Sveri or Eric or Gustav."

"Where is Bethlehem, anyways?"

"Isn't that a church in Spalding?"

Of course, Joe didn't say anything about the appearance of the angel.

We proceeded across the clearing in the same direction the Angel had gone. Ingmar and me tried to muster up our own rendition of the Norwegian national anthem, but Western Light expressed his depreciation by burying his head in a snowbank.

Finally, we arrived at a stavkirke (that's Norwegian for "old church") in a lonely field. As we entered, we noticed that there was a throng of Vikings with chiselled features and long hair standing quietly in the inner sanctum. They'd left their broadswords at the door, but they were all holding lefse sticks. And then they danced. It was the Dance of the Rosemalt Lefse Sticks. Let me tell you, it was something to behold – haunting is the word I'd use for it – anytime you get fifty Vikings in a stavkirke, waving lefse sticks above their heads!

When the Vikings' dance had ended, I noticed a cradle with a baby in it near the altar. There was a grand lady rocking the cradle.

"What should we do?" I whispered to Ingmar.

"Give him a present." Ingmar stepped up to the cradle and pulled a keychain from his pocket. "Keys to my fifty-nine Studebaker." I'd never seen Ingmar be so generous before, but maybe he had the Christmas spirit in him.

I was next. I reached into my pocket, thinking to offer the child some spare change. But what came out of my pocket was a full-sized duck decoy. "Here. A product of Saskatchewan. Carved it myself."

I tried to put on a good face, but I was a little ashamed of my gift. The real Wise Men offered Him gold and frankinstein and myrrh. But the lady rocking the cradle gave me a real nice smile and a chorus of angels burst out singing, and I knew that the world was unfolding as it should.

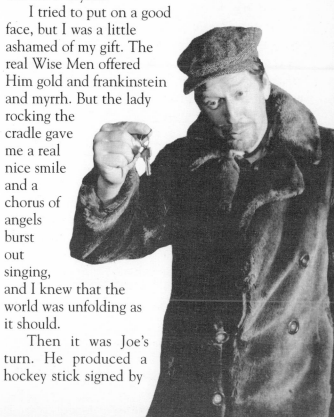

Then it was Joe's turn. He produced a hockey stick signed by all of the Saskatoon Blades. He pantomimed taking a slapshot and then he leaned the stick against the cradle. The baby giggled.

"Look," Joe said. "He's laughing." It was the first time I heard Joe say anything in thirty years.

The child's mother spoke up. "Go forth, and proclaim His birth to the world."

I woke up in my bed the next morning. I felt real strange. There was a knocking at my door. I put on my trousers and checked the pockets for duck decoys. I scrambled out of the bedroom and opened the front door. Ingmar Johannson was shuffling from one foot to the other on the icy step, fiddle case in hand. He'd come to play some Christmas tunes, he said, and he wanted me to accompany him on the piano. "Did you have sweet dreams last night?" he asked.

"Yup. The sweetest dreams ever I ever had."

"Duck decoy?"

"Yeah."

"Du, snakket Joe?"

"Yeah, Joe did speak!"

I still can't figure out why anybody'd dream a dream like that though.

Overhand Curling

and

Other Winter Sports

Handy Tips for Watching the Briar

NOT EVERYBODY THAT'S TUNING INTO THE Briar this year will have old Eddie Gustafson's expertise when it comes to understanding the game of curling. For the benefit of those folks who are new to the sport, I thought I'd put together a handy little guide to all the commonest plays and techniques that these Briar champions do. That way, I figure maybe everybody'll appreciate the game as much as old Eddie does.

There's a move that's common in my hometown, though I haven't seen it used here much, and it's called the thumb-between-the-knees polka. This moves usually occurs when the curlers are putting their rocks away at the end of the game. One of them accidentally gets his thumb slammed between two twenty-pound pieces of granite. When that happens, he generally puts his thumb between his knees and hops around like a gopher with his tail caught in a trap. Sometimes he sings a little song to go along with his dance. (I'd sing it for you here except it's got some nasty words in it.)

Then there's the old keel-over-at-the-hog-line move. You see this one quite a bit when you're watching curling on the tube. The skip glides himself outta the hack and he lets go the rock real smooth and then he just kinda keels over at the hog line and stares down at the ice for a good long time. Most people think that maybe he isn't too proud of the shot he just made, but that's not it at all. No, you see, he doesn't get up offa the ice right away cuz he can't get up. He's drunk half a bottle of aquavit the night before and he's got a temporary attack of what we in Saskatchewan call the runs. Don't worry, though, he'll just take some Alka-Selzer before his next shot and then he'll be right as rain.

Two of the commonest plays in curling is the out-turn and the in-turn. The out-turn is when you get waylaid coming home from the game and you end up in the beer parlour in Tisdale. Some individual that you never met before pukes on your parka, and when you get home your good wife turns you out. Or, as we say in the game of curling, she gives you the old out-turn. Then there's the in-turn, which takes you directly to the pub in Star City (where the local icemaker spends his time – which accounts for some of the discombobulating bumps in those sheets of ice in Star City).

Speaking of icemakers, there's a play in curling that you often see, and it's called the Icemaker's Waddle. That's when the icemaker has just pebbled the ice – so it's slippery as the Regina overpass on number 6 highway in January – and he's forgotten to wear his trusty broomball shoes.

He's got to make his way back from the far end of the rink, so he steps out on the ice and his legs go out from under him and he's backside over teakettle, landing on his toque. He's usually a tad cross-eyed after that first tumble – if he's a good icemaker and the ice is as hard as the back of God's head, like it's supposed to be – and so he falls two or three more times before he's halfway to the waiting room. By then, his hat's on all cockeyed and he's performing the Icemaker's Waddle. His feet are about two yards apart and his arms are stretched out for balance and he's generally muttering a prayer or else some unholy words.

There's also a curling technique you rarely see on TV or any other place, cuz it's only used in my hometown. It's called the Overhand Pitch. That's for when the front of the house is all blocked up with guard rocks and you got to make a takeout on the back of the four-foot circle. You rear back and toss the curling rock overhand so it clears those guards and comes bouncing into the house like a frozen road apple through a bobsleigh window. Amongst the folks back home, I've only seen Helga Arvinsdatter do the Overhand Pitch with any consistency and that's because she used to bench press her husband Arvin in the years before he met his Reward.

I sure hope this little guide to the game of curling helps you understand it as good as I do!

dessucnoC

S O THERE I WAS, CURLING MY HEART OUT in the final game of the Littlestone Home and Away bonspiel. Our skip Norman Johannson had just thrown his last rock, and I was sweeping for all I was worth to bring her into the house, when all of a sudden the hog line jumped up and bit me on the arse. Scared the bejesus out of me and the upshot was, my feet went out from under me and I went backside over teakettle, landing on the back of my head on the newly pebbled ice. Put a nice dint in her – the ice, I mean – and Egil Saandsbratten had to come out with some snow and hot water in order to patch the divot I made. The back of my head wasn't feeling none too good neither, although it was lucky that I was wearing my muskrat curling hat to cushion the blow.

Norman's brother Ingmar helped me up offa the ice and said, in that slow-talking way of his, "How many fingers do you see on this hand?"

I answered, "Four."

"Including the thumb?"

"Look, Ingmar," I said, "don't you remember I was there the day you caught your little finger in the bench saw?"

Norman came skidding up alongside. "You're

lookin' a tad cross-eyed," he said, "like you could lay on yer back and still see down a gopher hole."

"I'm all right," I said, "just a little shook up is all."

I couldn't curl right after that! I was bouncing rocks offa the side boards. We ended up losing the game and coming in second in the fourth event.

And for the next few days, I was able to do things backwards better than forwards. Listen to this: zyxwvutsrqponmlkjihgfedcba. You see what I mean? I sat down the one evening and read the entire Holy Bible back to front, right from the Apocalypse to Genesis. Ingmar called me an idiot savant. Whatever that means – but Ingmar said it was something good.

By the end of that week, I was sleeping all day and getting up just in time to see Peter read the news. I dried my face with a towel and then I washed it in hot water. I backed the baby blue pickup out of the shed and I didn't bother changing gears. I just kept her in reverse all the way downtown. I picked up the mail, went home and had a midnight supper. I lollygagged around the house and made a late dinner at two a.m. Then I spent the rest of the night working on my hobby – Freya Sorenson gave me a ship in a bottle for Christmas, and I was trying to get that ship out of the bottle, piece by piece. Round about six in the morning, I'd have a light breakfast and then I'd crawl into the sack.

Sounds a little goofy, mayhaps, but it made good sense to me.

Then last Sunday, I stayed up late enough to go to church. Preacher Nelson announced that we would sing hymn number 387. I opened the hymn book and commenced singing, "Kcor fo sega, tfelc rof em...."

Helga Arvinsdatter poked her elbow into my ribs. "Just what do you think you are singing?" she asked.

"Kcor fo sega," I said. "Hymn number 387."

"You have your book open to 783," she said sternly. "And it's not 'Kcor fo sega,' it's 'Rock of Ages.'"

Helga didn't embarrass me by making a big scene in church, but afterwards she got me into her car and drove me down to see the doctor in Watson.

"You bin concussed," ol' Doc Gudbrudson said. "Now you'll just have to lay in a dark room till you come to your right senses."

So here I am in the Watson Hospital, recovering from my concussion. Don't worry about me, though. It ain't so bad, specially now that I'm startin' to say my words right way round again.

Old Curlers

Y OU KNOW, YOU GOT TO HAND IT TO THAT Butch Berenson rink that curls out of North Battleford. Those guys is almost as old as I am, for crying in a bucket. If you put all their ages together and added them up and then went that far back in history, you'd end up in the time of the Viking stavkirkes.

Sometimes the lead Arne Arneson needs a little help getting into the upright position after he's settled in to the hack. They're living proof that you can sweep a rock into the house with a broom in one hand and a walker in the other. And they're also one of the best rinks in Saskatchewan (I'm not forgetting about Brad Heidt and the boys from Quill Lake now, because they're from out here in my neck of the woods, but they're still just a bunch of high-strung youngsters yet).

But you gotta like that Berenson rink on account of they show what old-timers can do when they put their mind to it. Oh sure, the spirit's willing and the body isn't sometimes, but it's the spirit that counts and the mental toughness. Those guys is so tough mentally that they could crack walnuts with their heads.

Me and my dog Great Western Light took a trip to Maymont once so's we could see the old boys play. It was a sight for sore eyes, let me tell you! That third Soren Bakke still uses a straw broom to sweep with, which is enough to justify offering him the Order of Canada, if you ask me. Not only is he a slick curler, he recycles farm products too. Well sir, their second Jim Arndt let go of a rock that was a tad on the light side, and I saw Soren go into his wiggly dance. That straw broom of his was slapping on the ice like the wings of a Great Blue Heron trying to take off of a northern lake. "Slap! slop! slap!" went the broom! "Don't treat me so rough," said the ice. By the time both Soren and the rock were at the far hog line, that particular sheet of ice had commenced melting like spring runoff had begun. Like somebody had accidentally turned the thermostat up to ninety-eight degrees. Like it was summer in the middle of winter. I was powerful afraid that he was gonna cause a flash flood with his vigorous sweeping.

In the next end, the skip, old Butch Berenson hisself, was faced with a grim shot. The other team was laying six and looked to win the game easy. But that didn't fizz on old Butch. No, cuz he had the hammer. He got his footing in the hack, took one baby step, and let that rock go. Didn't even slide with it or nothing. He just let her go, as straight and true as an arrow and twice as fast. I'm telling you, that rock didn't curl one inch between the time it left his hand and the time it hit the house at the other end of the rink. Faster than a speeding bullet. Knocked all of them six shot rocks outta there and then skidded over top of the hack at the south end of the rink, jumped the barrier, and made a nice curling-rock-sized hole in the wall. The icemaker from Maymont spent the better part of the next week looking for that rock and found it out in the middle of a farmer's field a quarter mile from town.

Them boys is something to see!

Curling Cheats

WELL, I AIN'T EXACTLY WET BEHIND THE ears! I've been running with the big dogs for some time now, if you know what I mean. But I learned a lesson in running with the big dogs when I curled against the Olson Twins, Ole and Axel, in the Littlestone Home and Away Bonspiel just last week.

Cheat! Let me tell you, those two guys make cheating into an art form! They're the Harry Houdinis of cheating! They don't actually need Snub Erixon and Ol' Joe Hogensund playing first and second for them, because they could win a bonspiel all by their lonesome, just so long as they could get away with their ragtag and bobtail shenanigans!

Me and my pal Norman Johannson and his brothers Ingmar and Joe was gunning for first in the first event when we come up against the Twins and their crew. We had glide in our stride and pep in our step. By the time the Twins were finished with us, we were four broken-down empty shells of men.

The ice was plenty fast last week, as it was real cold outside, and in the first end I saw Ole taking a wad of chewing gum out of his mouth and sticking it to the underside of his curling rock. That way, he could toss it down the ice with a hefty throw and that chewing gum would gather loose snow and bring the rock to a sudden stop. Me and Norman made three take-out attempts on that one rock after that, but it stuck to the ice in the blue ring just like it was anchored there with tent pegs.

At the top of the fifth end, the score was eight to six for them, we were lying three, and it was down to last rock. Axel did his special glide out of the hack – the first half of that glide is on his knee, the second half is balanced on the snoose tin in his back pocket, and the third half is lying flat on his belly. He didn't let go of his rock until he was almost acrost the hog line at the other end of the ice! And he drew right to the button!

Our slow-talking third, Ingmar Johannson, took real exception to this. "You was supposed to let go the stone a hundred foot back," he said. "Holy Gufflugenflegel!"

Now, you got to understand that the Twins is Swedish or Finnish or Icelander or something like that, and besides, they been living by their bachelor selves out in the Kitako back country for so long that they pretty much speak a language all their own which nobody else can understand. Axel turned to Ingmar and he said, "Glokkenspiel usdart snuffelig!" How are you gonna argue with a scategorical statement like that? Ingmar just shook his head and walked away.

So it was that we were down by four points

going into the last end. We were lying three, and if Norman could only draw in with his last rock, we'd tie her up.

"I'll show these scallywags a trick they maybe haven't learned yet," I said to Joe Johannson. I pulled a straw loose, so's it was sticking maybe six inches out of my broom.

Norman skidded out of the hack and let go his rock, and I could tell from the commencement that it was thrown too fast, but I just kept sweeping for all I was worth. Norman he was hollering at me, "No! No! Let it ride. Let it alone! Stop sweepin'!" but I kept pouring on the coals and I wouldn't stop – no, not for the world – until we was almost at the red circle and that straw come free of the broom and lodged itself underneath the rock and the rock screeched to a standstill right near the middle of the circle.

When the dust had settled, the Twins was both looking down at the damage and the score was tied. Ole was pointing at the straw sticking out from underneath that stone, and he was looking at me and saying, "Snorsbakken lutefisk hummeldinger," or something to that effect. Didn't make no difference to me, I couldn't make head nor tail out of him anyway.

Joe, he got so excited, he performed a little Strekkebokken polka, right there beside the Olson twins. Trouble was, he lost his footing on the blue circle and fell down and knocked two of our rocks right clean out of the house. The Twins laughed so hard they had to hold their bellies.

"Smorsbrod gufflugenflegel snurt," one of

them said. "We win by two."

Of course there was a big kafuffle after that and the Grand Master of the Bonspiel Gus Hammerdahl had to be called out. "The end was over," Norman told him. "We was just clearin' the rocks away."

"Had you made the measurement?" Gus asked.

"No."

"Had you marked up the new score?"

"No."

"Then the end wasn't over, gentlemen," he said. "We're playing by the traditional Scotch rules here."

So the Twins ended up winning the bonspiel for the fifth time in a row, and me and Norman and Ingmar and Joe was so heartbroke, we went on a losing streak and ended up a measly fourth in the third event.

That Time I Curled
in the Briar

🌿 🌿

MANY BRIARS HAVE COME AND GONE
since the beginning of time, or at
least since Ernie Richardson last was
here, and the record books are filled with all the
details like who threw up in the seventh end and
who wore the Scotch-tartan boxer shorts. But
one fact that you won't find in the record books
is that old Eddie Gustafson once played in the
briar, coming in to save the day for Saskatchewan
in general and for Rick Folk in particular.

Some people say I bear a strong resemblance
to old Rick – I guess it is possible for two real
good-looking fellas to come from one province –
and it was surely fate and diarrhea that got me
standing in for him. I had only come to watch
the final game, paid my money like all the rest of
the spectators, and I was sitting in the third row,
munching on some Hamburger Helper with my
dog Great Western Light. Couldn't help but
notice that Rick was a tad green around the gills
by the third end (he must have been into the
aquavit the night before), and in the seventh, he
come over to the gallery where I was sitting and
he said, "Eddie, I got a bad case of the diarrhea

and I don't dare squat in the hack. Think you could play this end for me?"

I got a tad green around the gills then too, thinking about all the pressure I was under, but then I heard myself saying, "Sure, Rick, sure, anything for an old Saskatchewan boy. What's the lay of the ice out there?"

"She's slopin' east," he said in a hurry. "Just hold the broom close to the rock, like this. I'll be back in two shakes of a mud hen's feathers."

So there I was, standing in the house at the one end of the rink, holding Rick's broom and calling for a takeout. The lights of the TV cameras were on me, my dog was setting there in the gallery with his paws over his eyes, and I was shaking in my toe rubbers. The rock come in a little on the light side and I was shouting "Hoot mon, hoot!" which is Scotch for "put the pedal to the metal."

That was okay, though, cuz I figured I could hold a broom just as good as the next man. But by the time it come down to skips' rocks, Rick still wasn't out of the washroom. I had no choice but to take the long lonesome walk down to the other end of the ice and settle into the hack.

My first rock didn't even clear the hog line, I was so darn nervous, and when it came time for me to throw the hammer, the other team was laying four and things were not looking too peachy. In order to win, I'd have to slide my stone betwixt two guards that were about six inches apart. I got together with my lead and I said, "Stall 'em, Jimmy, whiles I get something out of my baby blue pickup."

I came back a coupla minutes later with a carpenter's chalk line. "By my calculations," I told the boys, "if I do this right, the game is in the bag." I ran the chalk line from one end of the rink to the other and then I snapped her twice for good luck.

I settled back into the hack, and proceeded to curl, making a perfect glide towards the other end of the ice. I let go the rock and it turned and turned, grumbling along that chalk line like a bushy-eyed, cranky old farmer after a summer-long drought. I stood there with my mouth open as the rock dug its toes in and commenced stopping smack on the button.

The newspapermen's flashbulbs were apoppin' and when I looked over, there was Rick standing off to one side. "Nice shot," he said.

"How you feelin'?"

"Like I bin drug through a knothole backwards."

"Well, give her," I told him, handing him his broom back, "and play like you can."

And that's how I helped Rick and his team win the briar that year.

Preacher Nelson at Hockey

THERE WAS AN AWFUL SCANDAL IN MY hometown last week, involving the Lutheran minister, young Harold Tostbakken, and a hockey puck.

Preacher Nelson is a man of advanced years – he's almost as old as I am, for crying out loud – but he's a big man and in pretty good shape, having been a Mountie earlier on in his career. Used to be a mighty fine defenceman for the Carrot River Loggers too, or so I am told. But when we heard that he was planning to make his hockey comeback with the Littlestone Senior Men's Berserkers, me and the rest of the boys down on coffee row thought he might be a little long in the tooth.

Harold Tostbakken, on the other hand, is in his prime, just twenty-seven years old and a fine physical specimen.

The scandalous incident occurred down at the rink, during the first practice of the season. I'm only reporting hearsay now, but according to Helga Arvinsdatter, they were just getting started on a drill where three forwards come down the ice against two defencemen and try to score on the goaltender. Harold was leaning against the boards, and just before he took off with the puck, he was heard to shout: "Look out, old preacher man, cuz I can skate like the devil!"

Now, we all know that there's one thing you don't do to the Preacher – and that's to issue him a challenge. Because he's still got a mean streak in him a mile long, left over from his peacekeeping days, I guess. If you heard how he rattles the pews with his booming voice whenever somebody chances to fall asleep during one of his sermons, you'd know what I mean.

Well, Harold comes storming down the ice like a cat with tin cans tied to his tail. Just before he crosses the blue line, Harold drops the puck into his skates and begins to execute the Savardian Spin-o-rama – a neat little move that we've all seen him do a hundred times in league play. The Preacher was heard to chuckle at that moment, and then he cross-checked Harold across the face. Cut him for six stitches and knocked his two front teeth clean out of his head. As Harold lay bruised and bleeding on the ice, the Preacher skated by, smiling. Helga thought she heard him whisper something like "Get thee behind me, Harold."

When word got out about the Preacher's infraction, the whole town was up in arms. No minister of religion was supposed to behave that way, even if Harold was a smart aleck and even if he was asking for it. The church board had a meeting to decide if they should ask for the Preacher's resignation.

In the end, cooler heads prevailed, however.

It was reasoned that no preacher should behave the way that Preacher Nelson did but that, on the other hand, the Littlestone Senior Men's Berserkers were in desperate need of an enforcer, a big hunk of blue line. And the Preacher more than filled the bill.

So now the Preacher is saving his bone-crushing bodychecks for players on other teams, and the hometown folks are happy. All except for young Harold Tostbakken, that is, who refuses to darken the door of the Lutheran church for fear of a hard-hitting sermon.

The Puck Brings out the Darnedest Things in You

HEN IT COMES TO HOCKEY, THINGS never seem to change. That was made clear to me the other night, when I got talked into participating in an old-timer's pickup game, right here in my home community of Littlestone.

It was supposed to be just in fun, or so we were told, but there was fellas there twenty years older than me who were still taking the game pretty serious. Old Selmer Bakkenstedder is seventy-eight now, and he hadn't laced on a pair of skates since he got cut from the Saskatoon Sheiks back when Gordie Howe wasn't even thought of. He doesn't skate very smooth any more, but he can still stickhandle around the ice like the puck was Scotch-taped to his stick.

His main competition for the honour of being Oldest Man on the Ice was Egil Carlson – Spinner Carlson, we used to call him. He had a shot at the Leafs back in '48, and so he's not much younger than Selmer.

Those two fellas are neighbours out in the east country there, and on any other day of the week, they get along like a house afire. But get 'em on the ice together and they are as surly as two brown bears woke in the middle of hibernation season.

The antagonism started right at the opening faceoff. Egil made some untoward comment about Selmer's leather hockey helmet and how he looked like a World War Two aviator instead of a hockey player. Selmer let out a muffled chuckle, but I could tell he was irked. "Don't be goin' into the corner with your back turned," he muttered. "I'm playin' old rules hockey tonight."

Well, those two senior citizens were high-sticking, elbowing, tripping, and butt-ending the whole evening through – and they were doing some other things that they don't even have penalties for nowadays. Pretty soon, Egil skates into a corner with Selmer right behind him.

It was hard to say who got the worst of that encounter. Egil was bleeding from the nose, and Selmer was peeking through the earhole of his leather helmet. But they were both still standing when the sawdust and the iceflakes had settled.

And that's when the fisticuffs commenced. Egil shook his gloves off and caught hold of Selmer's sweater, tried to get it over top of Selmer's head. But Selmer wasn't having none of it. He reached out and grabbed Egil around the neck – he couldn't seem to get his old-time hockey gloves off because they were so tight and his seventy-eight-year-old fingers were so gnarled. It was like watching the replay of a fight between Max Bentley and Howie Morenz, only slowed right down to the speed of molasses in January.

And the longer the fight went on, the slower those two old-timers were moving. You could hear Egil's shoulders creak as he pulled his fist back in order to clobber Selmer one. Selmer saw the punch coming, of course – who wouldn't have? – and he ducked down out of the way at the speed with which a leaf falls from a poplar tree. Then Selmer took a swing and missed, his fist lumbering towards Egil's chin like the Goodyear blimp on its way to a football game.

There was no need for any of us to step in. After two or three attempts to swat one another, those two old-timers were plum tuckered out. That's when the rest of us decided it was time for a drink of aquavit. We took Selmer and Egil back to the dressing room, helped them out of their hockey equipment, and piled them into their separate half-tons for the ride back home.

The whole thing was forgotten in a few days, anyways. I saw Selmer and Egil in the Co-op Store a week or so later. They were laughing and jawing about how much fun that old-timer's hockey game was and how they both had to do it again soon.

But you want to know something? Things ain't gonna get no better betwixt those two old fellas, because they just keep getting meaner every year.

66 Skidoo

❧❧ ❧

THE LITTLESTONE AND DISTRICT ANNUAL Snowmobile Rally and Potluck Dinner was held last weekend. Kinda put me in mind of the first time I ever saw a Ski-Doo.

The year was 1966. Me and Norman Johannson were sitting in his shed by the pot-bellied stove. We'd told his good wife Barbo that we were gonna be out there making duck decoys. But the fire was too inviting and so was Norman's dandelion wine (which had just come of age). So we weren't doing too much of anything, just sitting there swapping stories, when we heard something roar into the yard that sounded like a cross betwixt a motor scooter and an airplane.

We went outside to take a look, and there was a contraption with skis on the front and caterpillar tracks on the back and young Joe Hoogeboom sitting on top of the whole affair, pleased as punch that his dad, Ole, had bought him the new machine. Joe couldn't a been more than seventeen at the time and full of devilment.

"Just come to show you my new Ski-Doo," he tells Norman. He's revving it up as we talk, for fear that it might stall and freeze up and never start again.

Norman gives that snowmobile the once-over and finally he says, "How fast she go?"

"I reckon ninety," says Joe, "but she ain't got a speedometer."

"Can she climb steep hills?" Norman asks.

"I been up and down every ditch in the territory," Joe says.

"How about showin' us what she can do up that hill right there?" And Norman points at a steep hill out behind his barn that I couldn't remember being there the year before. It's about a seventy-five degree incline up the one side. And Norman is giving me that cagey smile of his.

I didn't have time to warn the kid.

"Watch this," Joe says. He hits the gas and pops the clutch, and he's off like a shot up the near side of that hill and then he disappears over the top. All we hear is a "yahoo!" and then a scream and then the muffled thump of something heavy hitting six feet of snow at the bottom on the other side.

Well sir, we climb up that hill to see how the kid is doing. Only it isn't a hill at all. It's a bale stack with the snow blown in on one side to make it irresistible to young Ski-Dooers. On the other side is a sheer drop-off, twenty-five feet to the bottom. And there's young Joe Hoogeboom searching in the deep snow for his new machine that parted company with him somewheres in mid-air.

"You all right?" Norman hollers.

"How come you didn't tell me this was a bale stack instead of a hill?" the kid yells.

"Well, you made so much of that machine," Norman says, "I thought it could probably fly."

A Good Day

"IT'S BEEN A GOOD DAY," MY FRIEND Norman Johannson said as we were hitching the ice-fishing shack to the back of his Ski-Doo, out there at the Barrier Lake. "We caught our limits, we had us a fish fry, we drank a little homemade rat poison, and we ain't fallen through the ice once."

"Don't jinx us now," I replied, "by bein' too cocky." Norman fired up his snowmobile, and then he turned to me with a half-full jar of dandelion wine in his hand. "Here, one for the road."

"Yer fancy new ski machine idles a little on the fast side," I said.

"Yeah, it's the automatic choke. I gotta take it into Ingmar tomorrow and get him to set it proper."

I took a swig of Norman's wine, and he took a swig, and that's when we noticed that Norman's Ski-Doo was disappearing into the distance without us – ice-fishing shack in tow! We ran after the Ski-Doo as fast as we could, but it seemed like the automatic choke on that machine had been set by some cynical snowmobile repairman to go exactly one mile per hour faster than a fifty-six-year-old man can sprint in a snowmobile suit.

Only my dog Great Western Light was able to keep up with Norman's rig. But Western Light doesn't know much about driving snowmobiles. He just thought it was a good time – barking and nipping for all he was worth!

The Ski-Doo was proceeding in a lazy arc around the north end of the lake with Norman and me in hot pursuit. "This runnin's for the birds," I huffed and puffed to Norman. "What say we go get the baby blue pickup, and then we'll track down that errant snowmobile."

It took us a good fifteen minutes to get back to the shoreline, where the truck was parked. Norman stood on the running board of the truck, and I drove out on the lake. "You mosey up alongside the Ski-Doo," Norman shouted. "I'll leap on to the seat like a cowboy stoppin' a run-away horse." (Norman was feeling his oats by this time.)

Well sir, I steered us up next to the moving Ski-Doo, and Norman let out a holler and leaped for the seat of that machine. Ker-plunk! He was a little late with his jump, and so he landed face-down on the not-so-soft mid-winter ice.

I stopped the truck and got out to help Norman up. He dusted himself off, and then he grinned and said, "We'll try her again. I'm just gettin' the knack of this cowboy business."

Norman found his position back on the running board, and we started off in pursuit of that Ski-Doo again. We motored up beside it and Norman let out another "yee haw!" and then he jumped. Splat! This time he was a little early, landing in front of the Ski-Doo. I looked out my rear-view mirror just in time to see the back end of the snowmobile go over top of Norman. The ice-fishing hut slid over him too, coming back down to the ice with a solid thwack. For a minute, there, I was worried that that expensive fishing hut was going to be damaged.

Norman was a little worse for wear as a result of that little altercation between man and machine. After I got him to a sitting position, he commenced massaging his left shoulder. "That hurt," he said.

"You know what?" I told him. "That Ski-Doo seems to be goin' round and round us in a circle. I'll betcha that if we stayed right here, it'd come by again in five or six minutes. And then we could just jump on her as she goes by."

Sure enough, that snowmobile came by again. Norman had recovered from his injuries enough to climb onto the seat as it passed. He drove up on shore, and turned the key off. "We shoulda thought of that earlier," I told him when he'd gotten into the half-ton.

"It's funny what you don't think of when you've had too much dandelion wine!" Norman sputtered.

I Go for a Swim

WE WERE ON OUR WAY TO THE VILLAGE OF Île-à-la-Crosse one time – me and my dog Western Light in my baby blue pickup – for a little bit of ice fishing. It was the first day of January, and I thought to myself as we were coming out of Green Lake, "I wonder if the ice road is open this early?" You can save yourself half an hour off the trip if you take the ice road.

Sure enough, when we got to the edge of the lake, there was my good buddy Lorrie Arnott on the village grader clearing a path across the ice. I decided I was going to be the first traveller using the ice road that year, so I pulled off the highway and followed the grader across the lake.

Me and Western Light were having a little chit-chat about the price of rice in China when, all of a sudden, I looked up and there was no grader, no Lorrie, no nothing. Where did he go? Well, I found out soon enough, because the ice had cracked in front of me and we went through the same hole my friend Lorrie had gone through with the grader.

Down and down we went. I looked at Western Light, he looked at me, and nobody said nothing. Down and down. It's a deep lake.

We finally hit bottom – bang! – it's solid rock at the bottom of Lac Île-à-la-Crosse. I could see the grader down there beside us and Lorrie in the grader. The water's up to his eyeballs, and he's prying on the door handle and looking none too comfortable. Finally, he manages to get the door open, and he swims for dear life.

Now, I don't know if you've ever chanced to go through the ice on a deep lake like that. If you have, you'll know that the pressure's so strong on the outside of the half-ton that you can't open your door or even your window until the cab's nearly filled with water and the pressure's equalized. So there we were, the water was up to my waist and it was cold water too, being January. We waited for what seemed like a long while. By the time the icy water was up to our necks, me and Western Light had our noses glued to the roof of that pickup, scrounging for every last bit of air.

"Ya ready, pup?" I says. The dog perked his ears. And then I popped the door handle and we swam for it, every man – and dog – for himself. I looked up, and there was just a sliver of light to swim for, but that sliver got bigger and bigger until I finally surfaced. There was Lorrie and Western Light, waiting to give me a hand.

At last, I was lying on the ice, and I looked up at Lorrie and asked him, "What are we gonna do now?"

"Well, whatever we're gonna do, we better do it fast, because these wet clothes are gonna freeze solid in about three minutes."

We took off running for town, which was about fifteen miles away. We hadn't run more than half a mile before my Ski-Doo suit froze in the bent-legged position. Have you ever run fourteen-and-a-half miles without straightening your legs? You tend to get kind of tired.

We finally made it into town, and the good nurses at the Our Lady of the North Hospital put us in a big vat of hot water. It was only a day and a half before our temperatures came back to normal.

I'll tell you, I've heard of those hot tubs in California and in Banff National Park, where you can drink margueritas and tell light-bulb jokes, but there was never a hot tub sweeter or more life-giving than that vat of boiling water which the nurses of Île-à-la-Crosse prepared for us.

The Ice-Fishing Dog

WE WENT OUT ICE FISHING ON THE BARRIER Lake three weeks ago, me and my good friend Norman Johannson and my talented dog Great Western Light. We chopped a four-foot-by-four-foot hole in the ice at the west end of the lake. We tied some fishing line to the windshield wipers of my baby blue pickup truck. We baited our hooks with preserved minnows. Then we sat and drank hot chocolate in the cab of the truck while the windshield wipers worked our lines up and down.

It wasn't more than fifteen minutes before the driver's side windshield wipers commenced twitching. "Lookee here," I said to Norman, "we got a fish already. I told you this new trick of tying the line to the windshield wipers was guaranteed." That's when I noticed that the electric motor which runs the windshield wipers was commencing to whir and smoke. The next minute, my windshield wiper was twisted away from the windshield and was pointing straight down the ice-fishing hole like a well-witcher's wand. And before I could put down my hot chocolate and get out of the truck, that wiper was torn away from the vehicle and it disappeared down the ice hole.

Not a pretty sight, and I knew this was a job for my ice-fishing dog Great Western Light. "Go fish, boy!" I shouted. With little regard for life and limb or for just plain keeping warm, that dog leaped into the hole and disappeared into the dark water under the ice.

Normally, Great Western Light can locate a fish that's tangled in line and have him back at the surface within thirty seconds. But this job was taking longer. I kept time on my pocket watch. Thirty-five seconds, forty, forty-five, fifty...and still he hadn't come up for air.

Norman got out of the truck and came and stood beside me, hot chocolate in hand. "Was that your dog I saw jumping down the ice-fishing hole?" he asked.

"You bet it was," I told him. "And that's just one of his many talents." I was still keeping time. Two minutes, twenty seconds...two minutes, thirty seconds...two minutes, forty five....

"How long's he been down there?" Norman asked.

"A coupla minutes."

"Isn't that just the kind of month it's been?"

Twenty minutes later, things were starting to look pretty grim. There was still no sign of my dog and no likelihood of him surviving. I almost gave up hope.

Well, actually I did give up hope. I turned and started back toward the truck. I was crossing over a thin patch of ice with no snow cover on it, when I happened to look down. There, peering back up at me, was my faithful dog. He had his nose pressed up into an air bubble under the ice surface, and he was catching his breath on his way to the opening.

I hurried back to the hole, knelt down, and put my face close to the water. And then I whistled, whistled like Roger Whittaker going back to old Durham Town. It wasn't long before Great Western Light came swimming up through the opening. I reached in and grabbed him by the forepaws and dragged him out onto the ice. He still had that jackfish in his mouth – no, he wouldn't let go for the world – and dangling from that fish was a little bit of line and on the end of that was my windshield wiper!

When I opened the door of the pickup and the hound scampered in out of the cold, Norman said he thought it was only cats that had nine lives.

"Only cats," I told him, "and one particular dog – the talented and daring Great Western Light."

The Troll of the Lake

IT WAS THE DAY AFTER NEW YEAR'S, AND MY head was pounding because of the seven glasses of aquavit that Norman Johannson had poured for me the night before. When you're all headachy like that, sometimes the best thing to do is to get active. So me and my dog Great Western Light packed up our gear and headed to the Jackfish Lake, near the Battlefords there, for a little bit of ice fishing.

I managed to drill a hole in the ice and to set up my fishing line, complete with a little sleigh bell that jingles whenever a fish is caught. And then I thought how good it'd feel to lay down right there on the ice and have a snooze. It's not every day that you get to nurse your hangover by pressing your forehead against a whole lake of ice.

I hadn't been asleep for more than ten or twenty minutes when I heard a sharp crack and felt the ice tremble and then tremble again. I looked up. A huge mound, with something green on it like moss, was growing out of the lake. Splinters of ice were hanging off it, but still I could make out the rough shape of a troll's face, with two yellow eyes that glowed like a coal-oil lantern in a homesteader's window. He rose slowly from his sleeping place in the lake, looking none the better for having been woke up from his long winter's nap. The skin on his hairy torso looked like wet rotting tree bark.

I was standing with my dog on an ice floe in the middle of the lake. "What do you want?" I shouted to the troll.

"Did you make any New Year's resolutions?" the big fellow asked.

"None to speak of," I replied.

"Then come with me." The giant troll grabbed me up in one wet hairy hand and began to carry me across the lake. My dog was barking, so the troll turned around and picked him up too.

We stopped at a cave in the middle of some bushes, and the troll let us down. He was busy writing something with a lump of coal on two long sheets of birchbark. Then he grabbed a piece of birchbark in each of his two hands and hid them behind his back. "Pick a hand," he said, "and I will tell you your fortune."

I pointed to his right hand, and he held it out to me, dropping the birchbark into my outstretched arms. It read: "The Troll of the Lake will eat you for his dinner."

"Now, just wait a cotton-picking minute," I protested. "That ain't exactly no fortune cookie. Let me have another pick." But it was too late. He dropped me and my dog into a smelly vat filled with grease and gravy. Then he deposited us into an oven the size of my living room, and before he closed the door on us he licked his lips and said: "When the oven bell rings, you'll be ready to eat."

Things commenced getting a little hot after that. Me and Great Western Light were trying to climb out of the vat, but the sides were too slippery. Finally, we just sat back down and stewed in our own juices. That's when the dog spoke up; it was the first time I ever heard him speak. "Holy cow!" he exclaimed. "I haven't been in this much trouble since I went into your grandma's living room with mud on my paws."

"Why am I so gullible?" I asked him. "Everyone knows you're not supposed to speak to trolls. You're supposed to run away from them." I've always been the same way – taken in by my great-aunt Inger who cheats at Norwegian whist, fooled by Ingmar Johannson who keeps selling me spare parts for my pickup truck that I'll never even use.

Just then, I heard a bell ringing and I felt the hot oven turn cold. I opened my eyes to find that I was still lying on the ice. The dog was licking my face, and the bell was jingling on the end of my ice-fishing rig, letting me know that there was a four-pound walleye on the other end of the line.

I got home that evening, and I made myself a late New Year's resolution: I'm not gonna talk to any more trolls this year, because I know they're just trolling for a good dinner.

Helga's New Year's Kisses

and other

Wintertime Pleasures

New Year's Kisses

EVERY NEW YEAR'S EVE, AS THE HOUR approaches midnight in the Littlestone Town Hall, we all join hands and sing "Auld Lang Syne." We count down the last ten seconds into the New Year, and then pandemonium breaks loose. Always, in the moments that follow, Helga Arvinsdatter seeks me out and plants an enormous and disgusting kiss right on my mouth.

You have to know Helga in order to understand why kissing her depresses me so. She's a woman of some prominence, you might say, size XXXL. When she puts a man in that sleeper hold of hers and then dips him to within inches of the floor, it kind of takes his breath away.

The other disgusting thing is Helga's false teeth, which are always jangling around in her mouth like a peanut in a shell. Helga is a walking advertisement for denture glue; she can never seem to keep her teeth in her mouth. A few years ago, she kissed me as ardently as a high school girl on lover's leap, depositing her dental plate somewheres near my left tonsil. When she had finished, I reached into my mouth and retrieved the dentures, handed them back to her, and said,

"Here, I think you dropped something."

"Oh, Eddie," she replied, "you're such a sweet man."

One time Helga caught me in that death hold of hers and gave me a real French kiss with a twist. I had to go outside afterwards and ask Ingmar Johannson for a slug of his chewing tobacco, both to wash away the taste out of my mouth and to banish the memory of what I'd recently been through.

This year, I decided that enough was enough. At three minutes before midnight, I excused myself from my dance partner, Freya Sorenson, and went and hid in the broom closet. I could hear the rest of them out there on the dance floor, having fun and singing "Auld Lang Syne." I could hear the countdown to midnight and then the sounds of hugging and kissing. And over the din of noisemakers and wheezing party whistles, I heard Helga's deep voice: "Where has that Eddie Gustafson gone off to now?"

A hush fell over the assembled multitude. I heard Helga's heavy footsteps as she searched the hall, opening and closing doors. Finally, she stopped in front of the closet where I was hiding.

"Little pig, little pig, let me come in."

"No! Not by the hair of my chinny chin chin!" I exclaimed. Helga grabbed the closet doorknob and pulled. I held on for dear life at the other side of the door. But it was no use. Helga is stonger than two men on a normal day, but when she's fired up, she can single-handedly lift the front end of a Buick off the ground.

"I'll huff and I'll puff and I'll blow your house down," she promised as she wrenched the door open.

I was like a cornered rat who would do anything to survive. I saw that Helga was off balance, so I let go of the door handle unexpectedly – just as she was pulling on it, hard – and she careened backwards across the hall and fell into a bunch of chairs and tables. Norman Johannson was the first person to Helga's side.

"I'd run if I were you, Eddie," Norman said. "She's out cold now, but you know she'll be in a bad mood when she comes to."

I went straight home after that, like Norman told me to, took a shower and went to bed. Folks tell me that Helga was on her feet again five minutes later and that she vowed to catch up with me next New Year's Eve.

But I'm thinking that I'll spend a quiet New Year's Eve at home, in the coming year, with a small glass of aquavit and my dog Great Western Light. I'll sit down at the kitchen table and compose my New Year's resolutions. I'll watch the Royal Canadians on the boob tube. At midnight, I'll shake a paw with my dog and then I'll go to bed.

It sounds boring, I know, but it couldn't be any worse than what Helga Arvinsdatter has in store for me at the town hall.

Electrical Underwear

WELL, INGMAR JOHANNSON'S BEEN AT IT again. He'd heard me complain once too often about how cold it was last January, so he went to work on his latest invention – electrical underwear.

He got ahold of a pair of regular Stanfield's longjohns and ran some copper wire through the fabric. Then he hooked the whole rig up to a battery pack, which you could clip to your belt or tuck into your back pocket if you had a mind to. Ingmar's electrical underwear ran on four rechargeable D-cell batteries, the kind you can buy at your local Co-op.

He gave me the prototype of his invention, claiming that it was my whining that had got him thinking along these lines in the first place. After I'd worn those electric longjohns for a week – and liked them – Ingmar called me on the telephone. "I've made an improvement," he said, in that slow-talking way of his. "Come back to my garage and I'll fix you up."

When I showed up in Ingmar's Hiway Garage, he presented me with a portable battery recharger, complete with AC adapter. "There," he drawled. "You can plug in to any electrical outlet that happens to be near where you're sitting."

I went to a snowmobile rally the very next day. When the rest of the local gents saw me standing there, all toasty and warm, they all wanted a pair of Ingmar's electrical underwear, too. Ingmar was kept pretty busy, since he wasn't exactly set up for mass production. But pretty soon, he'd supplied half the male population of Littlestone with his electrical longjohns.

Which was all very well until I was sitting in the waiting room of the local skating rink last weekend, indulging in a game of schmeer with Norman Johannson and his cousin Semi and Cookie Swanson. Since I was planning to play cards for the rest of the afternoon, and since an electrical outlet was close at hand, I decided to plug in my rechargeable electric underwear right there and then. I figured that I could have the benefits of staying warm and still keep my batteries at the ready.

But then Norman told a real good joke about a Norwegian, a Swede, and a codfish. I laughed so hard that I almost wet my trousers. Or maybe I was just sweating too profusely from the warming effects of my underwear.

The next thing I knew, those underwear started shorting out, causing the full force of 110 volts to surge through my body. My eyeballs commenced to twitch at a rate of ten twitches per millisecond. Then I got a nosebleed. And then I decided to try and make my way to the electrical outlet so as to pull the plug. The rest of the fellows were laughing pretty hard as I got up off the bench and headed toward the wall. They told me later that I was doing a dance which reminded them of a haywire robot that had been misprogrammed on some science fiction TV show.

I went home that evening and I decided to put away my electrical underwear until next winter, when my friend Ingmar has finally ironed all the bugs out of his new invention. Until then, I guess I'll just tough it out in my regular BVDs.

My Clairvoyant Dog

THE ONLY GOOD THING ABOUT BEING storm-stayed in your own home during these long Saskatchewan winters is that you begin to appreciate your dog's special talents. Just this winter, we were inside during a blizzard watching *Hockey Night in Canada* – me and my handy dog Great Western Light – when I thought I'd conduct a little experiment. I'd read in the *Reader's Digest* that some dogs have clairvoyant powers, and I decided that I wanted to see if that applied to my own mutt. So I tore two scraps of paper from a letter-writing pad, and I wrote "Edmonton Oilers" on the one scrap and "Calgary Flames" on the other. Then I put a dog biscuit on top of each scrap of paper, and I decided that whichever one the dog ate the biscuit off of first was going to have the name of the winning team on it.

Great Western Light didn't even give it a second thought. He just snatched the biscuit off of the piece of paper that said "Calgary Flames" and wolfed the biscuit down. And sure enough, the Flames won that night 3 to 2.

I was in the café a week later, and I was telling Norman Johannson about my dog's uncanny abilities. He said, "Wait a minute. I've had about two hundred gallons of gasoline stolen from that tank on my back forty over the past year. I've got a pretty good idea who the culprit is. But you don't suppose I could write some names down and see which one your dog picks?"

"Sure," I said, and we went back to my house to get the dog's advice. We wrote down four names on four different pieces of paper, put a dog biscuit over each one of them. "The first one he picks'll be the thief," I told Norman.

When the dog gobbled up that first biscuit, Norman stared at the name underneath it and murmured, "Well, I'll be darned. It wasn't who I thought it was at all." But that didn't stop old Norman from phoning the guy up, right there on the spot, and giving the villain a piece of his mind.

"Look," Norman shouted into the phone, "I just found out you've been stealing my fuel."

I could hear disbelief and belligerence coming from the other end of the phone line, and when Norman told the man that Eddie Gustafson's dog had fingered him as a crook, I heard a loud guffaw come through the receiver – even though I was halfway across the room.

After that, news of my dog's special powers spread quickly through the town. We got calls and letters about stolen horse blankets and computers, about buried treasure and unsolved crimes. But the sweetest letter we ever got was from a young bride-to-be. Let me show you exactly what she wrote:

Dear Mr. Gustafson:

I am engaged to be married to a young man named George Swenson. I am concerned about the future. Will we be happy? Will we be rich?

Yours truly,

Kristiana Hogdebo

I was coming out of the Credit Union a few days later, and who should I run into but young George Swenson himself. He looked like he was under the weather. At last he said, "Mr. Gustafson, I understand your dog received a letter from my fiancée a while ago. I was just wondering – you know how important this is to me – I was just wondering how the dog was planning to respond?"

"Well, that's up to the dog, ain't it?"

The boy looked like I'd just dropped a Ford Aerostar on him. "I'd gladly give you fifty bucks," he said.

"Stop right there," I told him. "That'd be like takin' a bribe, and my dog don't take bribes."

When I got home and was in the middle of my lunch, I started thinking about those two lovebirds. I've known both of those kids since they were about three and a half, and if ever there were two people made for each other, those two are it. She's already finishing most of his sentences, and he teases her about everything under the sun. And they can hardly keep their hands offa each other.

So I got out a piece of paper and I wrote: *"The*

dog says 'yes.' Marry the boy, by all means. Signed, Eddie Gustafson."

George Swenson and Kristiana Hogdebo were married on January fifth. You never saw a happier couple than those two as they schottisched around the Littlestone Town Hall on their wedding night.

Upsought

E SUFFERED THROUGH A BLIZZARD HERE last week. Kinda reminded me of the snowstorms the old ones used to talk of, when they had to tie a rope betwixt the house and the barn, or when the kerosene lantern burnt out in the tarpaper window of the sod shack and the old homesteader couldn't find his way home.

These Saskatchewan blizzards are not to fool with.

But there we were, me and Norman Johannson and my dog, Great Western Light, on our way home from watching the senior hockey team play in Lake Lenore. Couldn't see the hood ornament in front of the windshield, the snow was so thick. Coming at us like meteorites and hemorrhoids as we made our way out of town.

I know. We shoulda turned back. We shoulda spent the evening in the Lake Lenore Hotel, taken a room and stayed the night. But nah. It was only twenty miles home, we figured. What could go wrong?

We turned off the blacktop, on to the grid road heading east to Littlestone. The snow was up around the hubcaps of the vehicle, and you couldn't differentiate between the road and the ditch because there were no car tracks. Nobody else was fool enough to be driving that night, I guess.

Norman was just pouring a cup of coffee out of his Thermos when my front tire on the driver's side slid into the ditch. I tried to crank her back up on the road, but the rear end of the truck swerved into the ditch sideways. And the next thing I knew, we were sitting there upside down, the motor still running and the radio still tuned to Lester Sinclair. But even Lester didn't have no ideas how we were gonna get out of that situation.

Lucky we had our seatbelts on. Great Western Light was licking my face. And Norman was covered in hot coffee, saying some bad words.

"What do we do now?" I says to Norman, half in shock.

"Well, first thing you could do is shut the motor off. I don't think we're goin' anywheres tonight."

We were buried in the snow, of course, right down to the door handles. So Norman opened a window and commenced digging. By the time the three of us were able to crawl outta that upturned vehicle, the snow was so thick that you wouldn't have been able to see a yardlight fifty feet away. And there was no sign of oncoming traffic.

So I suggested to Norman that we hole up in the truck for the night, wait for the snowplow to come and dig us out in the morning.

At first, that didn't seem like an attractive solution. But once we got back into the truck, I pulled my emergency kit from under the seat and opened it up. I had twenty-seven candles and three tins of canned heat – enough to keep us alive in a tent on Mt. Everest. But no matches!

Then I remembered using them matches to light a fire in the rain at Barrier Lake last summer.

And then I remembered the cigarette lighter. Well sir, after one or two tries, we got them candles burning and they heated up the cab of that truck nice and cozy. Kinda reminded me of a Lutheran church at Christmas.

Norman's good wife Barbo had packed a lovely lunch for us. Turkey sandwiches and mandarin oranges and lemon meringue pie in Tupperware containers. Great Western Light ate his share up like a good fellow and promptly went to sleep. Norman and me, we reclined in the upturned cab of that truck and traded stories of the past, the present, and the future.

Just as daylight was breaking, Norman said, "You know, we'll have to roll your truck more often. Don't get many chances like this to have a good old-fashioned confab, do we?"

Well, the snowplow did come, and some farmers drove out to help us tip my baby blue pickup back on to its tires. And we drove into town, and Arne Olson at Arne's Autobody agreed to pound out the dints for fifty bucks.

But that's fifty bucks well spent, I'd say, when the snow's falling outside and you can have a candlelight dinner with your favourite friend and your favourite dog.

Telmer Anstensen

TELMER ANSTENSEN DIED THIS WINTER. He was the last of the old ones. He'd come here from Iceland in the thirties, when his father's cannery and shipping company went belly up. So he arrived in Littlestone with no English and no prospect of a job. Ended up working in the blacksmith shop downtown until the shop closed in the late fifties. And then he bought some land in the back country, out there by Kitako Lake. Built a house so far from anywheres that the only way it could be gotten to was by boat or four-wheel drive or ice road in the winter.

One thing you learn, living in a Scandinavian community: you can make a blacksmith out of an Icelander, but you can never really take him away from the sea.

You'd see Telmer once a year, after he'd moved out to Kitako, when he'd come into town for supplies. The only person who heard from him oftener was Telmer's sister, Sigrid, who'd get a letter from him, scratched on brown paper, every month.

But the letters stopped coming last November, and Sigrid caught hold of me in church one Sunday and asked if I'd drive her out to Telmer's the next day. Something was wrong, she said.

So I put the chains on my tires, and we took the ice road across Kitako Lake to Telmer's place, me and Sigrid Anstensen and my dog Great Western Light.

The old man's cabin was in frightful disrepair. Windows broken. Firewood piled up in a heap beside the wood stove that Telmer used to heat the place. Scraps of food on a wooden table. But no Telmer.

I went outside and found Great Western Light digging in a pile of snow by the outhouse. And there was the old man's carcass, his spirit fled. His leathery face had a big grin on it as if to say, "You found me. Now what are you gonna do with me?"

We loaded him up in the half-ton and headed back to town, is what we did.

Sigrid asked me if I'd arrange the funeral, since she knew nothing about that sort of thing. I figured she didn't have any money to spare, and Telmer certainly had no head for finances, so I decided we'd have to bury him on the cheap. I phoned up Ingmar Johannson and asked him if that old hearse he sometimes drives for fun was back in working order. And it was. I got the Ladies Aid to organize a funeral lunch. And the local men pitched in to dig his grave out at the Lutheran cemetery.

It's a tricky business, this grave digging, partly because they've been burying people for seventy-five years out there without a map. People have been buried side by side, end to end, and even on top of one another. But the permafrost is the real big problem. We lit fires on top of Telmer's spot for a week, hoping to thaw out the ground. Five of us spent the better part of a day, with pickaxe and shovel, trying to dig the grave. But it was no use.

Finally, I had to call Sigrid and tell her that the burial was off. We'd have to wait till spring.

Then we had to decide what to do with the corpse. The undertaker didn't want Telmer's remains, since we weren't using his hearse at the funeral. Somebody suggested that we keep him in the freezer room at the local meat market, but Rusty the butcher thought that'd be bad for business. And then Ingmar Johannson came up with the bright idea of storing Telmer's body down a well or a cistern. So we took the corpse out to Norman Johannson's place, tied a rope around Telmer's ankle, and lowered him into the well in Norman's barn.

"Don't worry," Norman said. "He'll keep real good down there."

And here we are, waiting for spring so we can let the old guy rest in peace.

Norman told me, the other day, that he was out there pumping water for his cattle when he heard a noise coming from deep down in the well. He stopped and listened. He said he coulda swore it was a laugh or a chuckle coming from down there. Norman gave his head a shake and was about to start again, but he heard a whisper in his ear. And he swore to me that it was Telmer's happy Icelandic voice, as he'd last heard it several years ago. And it said two words. It said, "Ship ahoy!"

Blizzards

WHEN IT'S NEAR CHRISTMAS AND THE snow is lying on the ground, people is always talking about the blizzards of yesteryear. And I say that there's nothing happened in the last forty-odd years that's been a patch on 1952 for snow and cold and general discombobulation.

I was just a wisp of a thing back then, of course, but I can still remember having to put on snowshoes and then climbing out the dormer window on my Norwegian grandma's two-and-a-half-storey farmhouse in order to wend my way to school. Later on that year, we dug a tunnel under the snowbanks all the way from my grandma's house twelve miles into town. So I didn't even have to go outside to get my education.

And blizzard! I tell you, there was a blizzard in November of 1952 that we're still recovering from out here in Littlestone. I remember old Egil Torvinson tied a rope betwixt his house and his barn so's he wouldn't get lost in the event of snow blindness. Well, old Egil got discombobulated in the middle of that November snowstorm and he lost his sense of direction. Somehow ended up following the path of his barbwire fence around a full section of land. Got lost out on the baldhead prairie, and nobody found him until the snow melted the next spring. I tell ya, old Norwegians must have ice flowing in their veins because when they thawed old Egil out, he come to and started yammering on in Norwegian about what a snowstorm that was and had he been sleeping long and did he miss Christmas and was there any lutefisk left? He was the first guy I know of who was ever froze cryogenetically (or whatever they call it) and who came to afterwards.

It was so cold that winter, I remember they used to give us kids booster shots with some kind of antifreeze in them so's we wouldn't freeze up altogether. A little-known fact is that you usually freeze from the ground up out here, on account of the circulation is poorest the further away you get from your heart. When the grown-ups noticed us kids starting to plod around kinda wooden-legged, they would take a spoon and tap on our feet and ankles and shinbones. "Yup," they'd say, "frozen right the way up to the knee." And then they'd send us off to crusty old Doc Gudbrudson for a booster shot filled with antifreeze.

Why, it was in 1952 that my dog outran an Edsel that was going fifty miles an hour along our grid township road. You see, the dog went out to chase the car and, just then, a cold spell hit and froze both the dog and the car up solid. They just remained out there on the road all winter long, like two frozen ice sculptures that you might see on a visit to the city, until the next spring when the thaw hit. The dog thawed out first, of course, and that's the reason he outrun the Edsel.

There's some places out in the back country west of Kitako where the snow still hasn't melted from those big snowstorms back in '52. It just formed itself into a glacier and, I'm told, it's moving this way at a rate of two foot per year. By the year 3000, we're expecting it to cause another ice age.

Nosirree, boys, if you're talking of snow and cold and blizzard, there'll never be a year again that was a patch on 1952.

Once in a Blue Moon

NORMAN JOHANNSON AND HIS GOOD WIFE Barbo packed up the car and headed for BC this January. Their son Sten Ove has been working in a lumber mill in Port Alberni for the past three years, and he'd invited them to pay him a visit. They asked me if I'd check in on their home place once in a blue moon, to make sure that everything was in order.

I soon found out that "once in a blue moon" means something different to them than it does to me.

The day before they left, they presented me with a list of things to do. I had to check the furnace filter and make sure that the furnace was cutting in at the right time. I had to flush the toilet and make sure it wasn't gurgling. I had to check the fusebox to make sure that no fuse had blown. I had to go out in the backyard and make sure that the septic tank was running. I had to start up the Allis Chalmers and throw the cows a round bale once a day. I had to make sure the water trough wasn't freezing over. And, most important of all, I had to water the plants that Barbo had scattered about the house. She told me the plants prefer it if you sing to them while you're watering. I said I hoped they liked "Good-night Irene," since that's the only song I know all the words to.

Norman and Barbo left on the morning of January third. That afternoon, me and my trusty dog Great Western Light jumped into the baby blue pickup and headed out to Norman's for a routine check.

I didn't even have my key in the doorknob when I sensed that something was wrong. I could hear the sound of water running in the house. I went downstairs, and sure enough, the septic tank was backing up into the basement. Lucky I had my rubber boots on.

I found a pail and a mop and started cleaning up, and then I heard a pop and a bang, and I felt a mist of cold water on the back of my neck. The outside faucets hadn't been turned off, and a copper pipe had frozen and burst! I had a roll of hockey tape in my coveralls, so I wound that tape around the pipe and stopped the flow of water as best I could.

Then I phoned Charlie Hushagen, the plumber.

It was midnight before me and Western Light returned home that night. We hopped into bed and, let me tell you, we slept fast.

The next afternoon, we headed out to Norman's again, thinking to nip any oncoming disasters in the bud. Well sir, the pilot light in the furnace had gone out. The place was freezing. Took me three hours to get everything back to normal. And then I noticed a faint odour of natural gas in the house and I had to bring in the guy from SaskEnergy in Melfort.

What more could go wrong? I asked myself. But the next day it was twenty-seven below outside and I couldn't get the tractor going. Had to roll a twelve-hundred-pound round bale across the yard by hand. The sweat was freezing before it even got a chance to run down my armpit.

Every day after that, it was something else. A tree fell on the power line and I had to get that fixed. I checked the rods in Norman's bins and found that some of his grain was heating up. I had to auger it out on to a tarp on the ground. Then one of Norman's Charolais cows got the croup. I was on the phone to the vet every day after that, figuring out what medicine to give the cow and how to administer it.

Norman and Barbo got back three weeks later, looking well rested, even despite such a long and faraway sojourn. Barbo waltzed into the house, took one look at the African violet drooping on her kitchen counter, and said, "Eddie, you killed it. Didn't you check on the place at all while we were away?"

Sturle and Knud at Schmeer

ME AND THE BOYS AND MY DOG GREAT
Western Light thought we was gonna
be without a place to play cards when
the local poolroom closed earlier this year. But
when we moved the card table and the shuffleboard over to the waiting room of the curling
rink, we realized we'd found a new home.

What's so special about the curling rink in
wintertime is that there's bonspiels practically
every weekend. And when the bonspiel's on, the
Ladies Aid fires up the stoves in the booth at ten
every morning and keeps us supplied with hot
coffee and hamburgers all day. They've even
taken to bringing in their old soup bones for
Great Western Light to gnaw on in the corner.

A coupla months ago, Norman Johannson
and me were in there, playing schmeer at two bits
a game and ten cents a hickey with two old-
timers from the level one home down the road –
Knud Hoeppner and old Sturle Sturleson. Now,
Knud and Sturle don't get along very well, never
have. I'm told their antagonism started back in
the 1940s when Sturle plowed up the road
allowance between their two farms. They never
ever kissed and made up, those two, and some

quirk of fate ensured that when they retired, they'd have to live next door to one another in the old folks' home.

So there we were, playing schmeer, and after the first hand, Knud criticizes Sturle for leading with diamonds when his strong suit was hearts. Sturle starts calling Knud bad names under his breath. A few minutes later, Knud shoots the moon on an ace and an eight – and of course he doesn't make it. Well, Sturle throws his cards in the air, grabs his walker, and heads outta the rink. But before he leaves, he looks Knud straight in the eye and shouts out, "Sløsken!" – which is a bad word in Norwegian – at the top of his lungs.

This is pretty usual behaviour for those two, so Norman and I didn't think anything of it.

But two weeks later, Sturle and Knud were playing shuffleboard together when Sturle accused Knud of cheating. So Knud picks up a shuffleboard rock and fires it at Sturle as hard as he can throw, and then the fight was on. There was hair-pulling and throat-squeezing and snoose flying in all directions and, by the time Norman and I got between them, those two octogenarians were rolling around on the linoleum.

Norman and me got to thinking that enough was enough, so we decided to get involved. That night, we sat down and composed a letter, had Norman's wife Barbo type it up for us. It went:

Dear friend:
    I apologize for bein' so hard to get along with all these years. Enough is enough. I've

always thought of you as a Prince of a Man,
and as a token of my friendship, I want to
buy you dinner. Please come to the Chinese
café at six o'clock on January tenth, and I'll
shake your hand.

Yours truly,
and so forth.

And so we mailed that same letter to both
Sturle and Knud.

You can bet that at six o'clock on the tenth
of January, Norman and me were sitting on some
stools at the local café. First old Sturle shows up,
looks around kinda shiftily, and asks for a menu.
Then Knud walks in, offers Sturle his hand and
says, loud enough for everyone to hear, "You
know, I'm changin' my opinion of you already.
Let's eat!" Well sir, they both order the most
expensive things on the menu, because they each
figure the other guy is buying. So they eat up and
have a whale of a time, telling jokes and sharing
memories. When it comes time to pay, Sturle
looks at Knud and Knud looks at Sturle and they
both look at the bill, sitting there between them
on the table. They make some small talk for
awhile, and then Sturle says to Knud, "You did
promise to pay, didn't ya?"

"Now just hold on for one minute here,"
Knud says. "You're the one that's payin'."

"Wait a minute now," Sturle says. "What
about this here letter?" And he pulls a wrinkly
piece of paper outta his cardigan pocket.

"That's what you sent me," Knud says – and

he pulls the identical letter out of his vest.

This was going nowheres fast. So finally Norman steps in and says, "Me and Eddie wrote that letter, and it was only to see if you old codgers could get along for a minute or two. And you did. So don't spoil it."

Well, Knud and Sturle still hem and haw about one another around the card table, but they don't fist fight no more. They spend most of their time now worrying about some trick they're expecting me and Norman to pull on the both of them.

Norman and Me Do the Strekkebokken Polka

NORMAN JOHANNSON AND HIS GOOD WIFE Barbo love to dance. So it came as no surprise to me when I heard that they'd entered their names in the Sons of Norway strekkebokken polka competition that was held in Weldon this past November.

Once he'd allowed his name to stand for the competition, Norman spent most of his days down in the basement with his wife, practicing his footwork to an Olaf Sven polka record. You couldn't get him out of the house for love nor money. Not even the promise of a good day of duck hunting would tear him away.

"Nah," he'd say, "I'd better practice my glide and my handhold."

"But Norman, duck hunting season don't last forever."

He put his hand on my shoulder as if to confide in me. "It's been a lean year, Eddie," he said, after some deliberation. "I'm depending on that fifty-dollar prize money so's I can buy my wife a nice Christmas present."

Well, there's no arguing with the need to buy your wife a nice Christmas present, so I decided to leave well enough alone.

Which was fine until it was two days before the big dance competition and Barbo came down with a vicious flu bug. I got a phone call from Norman that morning. He sounded sort of discombobulated. "You know I'm relying on winning that prize money," he said to me.

"Yeah? So?"

"So I was wondering, Eddie – there's no one else, ya see – I was wondering if you'd be my dance partner."

"Yer dance partner!"

"I don't have no sisters, you see, and Barbo's awful jealous lest I dance with any other woman."

"Couldn't you ask one of your brothers? What about Ingmar?"

"He's too big and clumsy."

"Well, what about Joe?"

"Too shy. He'd never survive the experience. Eddie, you gotta help me – ya know I need the money."

That's how I found myself, the next afternoon, in Norman's basement, practicing the Strekkebokken polka. Barbo was reclined nearby on a ratty old sofa, sniffling into some Kleenex and then stuffing it into the pocket of her housecoat, and offering advice.

"Why do I have to be the lady?" I asked finally.

"Because you're shorter than Norman," Barbo explained. "Now let him have the lead, Eddie, but don't grab him around the neck like you're wrastling with a calf."

It was Norman and me who drove to Weldon for the competition that Saturday evening. "You nervous?" Norman asked, as we pulled into town.

"Yup."

"Well, just remember that dancing the Strekkebokken polka is like riding a bicycle – you never forget how."

We summoned up all our courage and went into the hall just as the polka competition was beginning. There were a few titters when Norman and me slipped off our toe rubbers and commenced dancing. But you can bet your bottom dollar that the tittering stopped when they saw that Norman and me could Strekkebokken polka with the best of them. We could see out of the corner of our eyes that one other couple was pretty good too. They were a little on the geriatric side, but the little guy could kick pretty high in the air for an eighty-six-year-old. And his chubby wife went jiggling around the dance floor with obvious good humour, like a big bowl of red Jello. But that only spurred us on. We whirled and twirled and jigged and hopped on one foot and then the other like one-legged cowboys in a butt-kicking contest.

It goes without saying that we were sorely disappointed when they announced that we had come second in the competition. Especially since there were only two couples entered. It was a long drive home, after that, since second prize was a pair of rosemalt oven mitts. Norman was sincerely depressed by the time he dropped me off at my house. "The real kicker," he said, "is havin' to inform Barbo that all our practicing was for naught."

"Well, winnin' ain't everything," I replied, getting out of the car. "We tried our level best, and that's all that's expected of a man when he's dancing the woman's part."

Hedda Gabler

AS SOON AS THE TREE IS CHUCKED INTO the back alley and Christmas is over, the folks in my hometown start thinking about things they can do to make the long winter pass more quickly. This year, we decided to create the Littlestone and District Annual Henrik Ibsen Theatre Festival, produced and acted by us. We had a town hall meeting where we settled on a play called *Hedda Gabler*, an uplifting little number about a housewife who can't tolerate being alive and so she puts a pistol in her mouth and fires it. Just the right cure for the lack-of-light syndrome that weighs us all down at this time of year.

Freya Sorenson agreed to play the part of Hedda (just so long as we could assure her that the gun wouldn't be a real one), and Ingmar Johannson and me volunteered to build the setting. That way, Ingmar could show off his famous inventiveness, and I could show off my little-known carpentry skills.

The genuine Norwegian hytte, or holiday cottage, that we created – right there on the town hall stage – was a sight to see. It featured two-by-six construction, complete with working lighting fixtures and, yes, a kitchen sink. For the final moment of the play, we pulled out all the stops. Ingmar drilled a hole in the back wall and pushed some rubber tubing through it. On the backstage end of the tubing he attached a squeeze bottle filled with beet juice. Freya was supposed to back up to that hole at the right moment; she was supposed to place the toy gun in her mouth and pull the trigger. Meanwhile, behind the scenes, I was supposed to fire off a starting pistol that we'd borrowed from the high school physical education instructor. Freya would bang her head backwards against the wall, Ingmar would squirt out the beet juice, and then Freya would fall face down on the floor, revealing that the back of her head was covered in what they call stage blood.

It worked smooth in the rehearsal.

Then came the opening night. All the townsfolk, and even some visitors, had gathered in the Littlestone Town Hall, waiting for our much-ballyhooed special effect. The show went like a house on fire, with Freya and her friends cavorting around the stage – laughing and bawling and kissing and hugging – like a bunch of movie stars.

Then come the high point of the play. The audience gasped when Freya backed up to the wall and put the toy gun in her mouth. Somebody shouted, "Don't do it!" but it was too late. She pulled the plastic trigger. Behind the scenes, I squeezed the trigger on the starting pistol too. Click! It didn't go off. I pointed it at the floor and tried to fire again – nothing happened. Finally I did the only thing I could think of to do. I shouted out "Bang!" at the top of my lungs. Freya had the presence of mind to bang her head against the wall just then, and Ingmar squeezed the beet juice out of the squeeze bottle. Trouble was, Freya had misjudged where the hole was by a good six inches, and beet juice went flying across the stage and out into the audience, where it landed on Helga Arvinsdatter – or more particularly on her new fur coat.

Still, the people of Littlestone are not an overly criticizing bunch, and they gave us all a standing ovation at the end of the spectacle. A week or so later, though, Helga Arvinsdatter caught ahold of Ingmar and me at Jolly's Café and asked us when we were going to pay her dry cleaning bill.

I guess the theatre is an expensive business to get involved in.

The Winter Carnival

WE DROVE UP TO THE WINTER CARNIVAL in Prince Albert this February, me and my talented dog Great Western Light. Had some pancakes with a few of the local trappers and radio personalities, and then we headed into the Great Out of Doors for the annual dogsledding competition.

Norman Johannson's cousin Einar is a conservation officer up north, and he usually enters a dog team in the race. Western Light and I went over to the starting line to have a word with him, but he was looking pretty down in the mouth. "My lead dog, Thor," he complained, "has just come down with a bad case of the bronchial pneumonia."

I made some lame joke about him borrowing Western Light if he had a mind to. Einar stood there for a long time, squinting at my dog.

"Looks like a strong animal," Einar says. "Does he understand what 'mush' means?"

"Einar," I said, "that dog's so smart, I been givin' him books in Roman history to read."

"Will you lend him to me for the day?"

I looked at Western Light, and he looked at me as much as to say, "Put me in, Coach."

I couldn't help but notice, as we were putting the harness on him, that Western Light was eyeing up the lead dog in the sledding team next to us. She was a well-built little mutt, maybe a cross between a husky and a wolf, standing next to him on the ice. It didn't take no rocket scientist to see that she'd fanned the flames of love in my dog's stout heart.

Lucky thing for Einar that Western Light was hopelessly attracted to the fastest lead dog in the race. They all lined up at the starting gate, and when the gun went off, that she-dog bolted like she'd just seen a rabbit and Western Light took after her in a rambunctious manner. Neither Einar nor his other dogs were prepared for it, and Western Light dragged the whole works of them for ten or fifteen yards before they all found their feet and started running in time.

At the halfway point of the race, Einar's team was tied for first place, with Western Light running beside that she-dog, every now and then nipping her on the ear like a schoolboy with a bad case of hormones.

I kept wondering how we was going to coax my dog to win the race outright. Then I remembered the box of Hamburger Helper that was in the glove compartment of my baby blue pickup. You could take all the she-dogs in the world and leave them barking on the front step, and Western Light would ignore them if he had his plate of Hamburger Helper in front of him.

I went to the supermarket and bought some hamburger meat and a can of propane. I set my camping stove up on the tailgate of my truck, right there at the finish line. I greased up a frypan and commenced cooking the Hamburger Helper.

That's when Western Light appeared on the horizon, neck and neck with that other dog. Both drivers were yelling "Mush!" at the top of their lungs and running hard behind their sleds. They were about two hundred yards away from the finish line when Western Light stuck his nose in the air and got a whiff of the meal I was cooking for him.

Well sir, he took off like he'd seen the Promised Land. The only trouble was, he ripped the stays right out of the harness and left Einar and his dogs stranded out on the ice in the middle of the North Saskatchewan River.

By the time Einar limped to the finish line, Western Light was just licking up the last of his meal. Einar wasn't sad, though. It had been a close race all the way, and it was the first time Einar's team had finished in the top ten.

One of the other drivers came and offered me six hundred bucks for my dog afterwards. I couldn't bear to part with the mutt, though. He just keeps showing me new talents every day.

Y2K?

ME AND NORMAN JOHANNSON AND HIS brother Ingmar were sitting in Jolly's Café this week, discussing the Y2K. Ingmar had read in the *StarPhoenix* that everybody was gonna be in for a heap of trouble and we'd better make a contingency plan.

"Y2K?" Ingmar drawled in that slow-talking way of his. "What is that?"

"Alls I know," said Norman, "is that Kay Nelson was comin' outta the Board Store with two bottles of cherry brandy under her arm. I said it to her then, and I'll say it now: 'Why Two Kay?'"

"It's somethin' about computers bein' discombobulated," I said.

"But there is only one computer in town," Norman argued, "and that's the one at the Credit Union. If it goes on the blink and they forget that I still owe 'em for that loan they gave me to buy the combine two years ago, I'll be real heartbroke."

Meantime, Ingmar was reading from his newspaper. "Says here she'll all go haywire on New Year's Eve."

"Won't fizz on me," Norman piped up. "I'm plannin' on cuttin' a mean rug that night."

"Says here the power might go out."

"Well, Eddie's got enough camp lanterns in his cellar to light the whole town up like a Christmas tree," Norman answered back. "Make sure you have some Duracells on hand, just in case, Eddie."

"Says here that the natural gas might run out."

"Well that's no problem. Eddie's got a coal-oil stove in his living room. Don't you still have that ol' coal oil you bought from Semi Bakkenstedder?"

"I do, but –"

"Well, we can go over to Eddie's if the natural gas runs out. Besides," he said, "if Eddie keeps feedin' that dog of his Hamburger Helper, he'll have enough natural gas in him to heat up the whole town."

"Says here the water supply might be cut off."

"Water schmater, it'll be New Year's Eve," chortled Norman. "And I happen to know that Eddie has been brewin' up a batch of his world-famous chokecherry wine. Just make sure there's enough for everybody, come New Year's Eve, eh Eddie?"

Ingmar said he thought that was a good idea too.

"Say," Norman went on. "Why don't we just have a big New Year's Eve Party at yer house, Eddie? It'll be nice and cozy. We could roll the carpet back and have a dance. And you had a good crop of potatoes last fall. The Ladies Aid could come and cook up enough lefse to last us right into the next ice age."

"Now hold on right there," I finally got a word in edgewise. "Yer already planning a party over at my place on New Year's Eve, but nobody's asked me what my plans are. What if I wanna be bringing in the new year at the Banff Springs Motel or something?"

"Come on, Eddie," said Norman. "You ain't gonna be doin' that. The cost of a motel room there must be at least fifty, sixty dollars a night." He turned to Ingmar. "You don't gotta worry none about no Y2K contingency plans, little brother. Our contingency plan is to go to Eddie's on New Year's Eve."

My New Year's Resolutions

IT'S TIME TO MAKE A FEW NEW YEAR'S resolutions so that this year will be even better than last year was.

I ain't gonna curl without toe rubbers again. Took me three weeks before I stopped seeing double after I slipped and fell on the ice this winter. And it sure draws people's attention when you sing "Rock of Ages" backwards in church after that.

I ain't gonna eat so much lutefisk next Christmas Eve that it bungs me up for three days afterwards. I ain't gonna feed my dog Great Western Light six extra bowlfuls of Hamburger Helper so that he gets bunged up too and we're both miserable. And I ain't gonna drink so much aquavit that I forget how to use the telephone and can't even call Doc Gudbrudson to get his advice on my upsought stomach.

I ain't gonna get kissed by Helga Arvinsdatter at the New Year's Eve dance. This year, she kissed me so hard that her dentures come loose and I dang near choked on them.

I ain't gonna participate in no more of Ingmar Johannson's crazy inventions. Those electric underwear of his were almost the death of me!

Now I hear he's working on a pair of spring-loaded rubber boots that are supposed to make you walk ten mile an hour or faster. (I'll have to report on them another time.)

I ain't gonna go into the Town Hall kitchen after the ladies have been cooking lutefisk no more. I almost didn't escape with my clothes on after the last time. Kinda brings to mind the Orvis Saga all over again.

I ain't gonna listen to no TV how-to programs any more. I particularly ain't gonna use potatoes to screw broken lightbulbs out of the Christmas lights. Last time I did it, I was deep-fried like a spudnut. It was enough to give a hibernating gopher the heartburn!

I ain't gonna accuse my Norwegian grandmother and my great-aunt Inger of cheating at Norwegian whist. Now they're telling me that they're not going to give me any more jars of their raspberry preserve unless I apologize first. And my great-aunt's stopped knitting me that cardigan she was working on. "It's work to rule," she says, "until you learn to respect yer elders."

I ain't gonna listen to no more trolls or huldrefolk this year (not even the one under my Christmas tree). They'll lead you down blind paths by the dozen.

I ain't gonna take the ice road across to Île-à-la-Crosse no more. I take my bath once a year, same as the next man, and I don't need to be baptized in freezy-cold water more than once. Besides, running bent-legged in a frozen snowmobile suit ain't my idea of good exercise.

I ain't promising to look after Norman and Barbo's place next year, while they're away on vacation, either. Not unless they can provide me with a troubleshooting phone list of all the plumbers, electricians, farm mechanics, and veterinarians in the area. And also a month-long supply of Extra Strength Tylenol.

I ain't gonna get involved in no Strekkebokken polka competitions with Norman next year – not unless I get to dance the man's part.

As a matter of fact, I'm gonna resolve not to do the same things that I resolved not to do last New Year's Eve. If I keep working at it, I just might get it right.

Until next time, this is Eddie Gustafson wishing you a happy new year from me and my Norwegian grandmother and my dog Great Western Light. And if you haven't made your New Year's Eve contingency plan yet, why don't you just come over to my place – seems like everybody else is gonna be there.

DWAYNE BRENNA was born in Spalding, Saskatchewan, and raised in Naicam. An actor and writer in Saskatoon, Dwayne is also head of the drama department at the University of Saskatchewan. Although this is the first time Eddie Gustafson's pearls of wisdom have appeared in print, Eddie's no stranger to radio listeners – Dwayne has been portraying him on CBC Saskatchewan since 1996.

The author would like to thank CBC Radio Saskatchewan, (and particularly Rob Southcott, who started it all), Angus Ferguson and Louisa Ferguson and Dancing Sky Theatre, Rocky Lakner, Elizabeth Anstensen, and, of course, Bev, Wilson, Eric, and Conner Brenna.